I0647919

MURDER
IN THE HAMPTONS

MURDER
IN THE HAMPTONS

JEANNE TOOMEY

SUNSTONE
PRESS

SANTA FE
NEW MEXICO

Copyright © 1994 by Jeanne Toomey

All rights reserved

No part of this book may be reproduced in any form or by any electronic or mechanical means including information storage and retrieval systems, without permission in writing from the publisher, except by a reviewer who may quote brief passages in a review.

Library of Congress Cataloging in Publication Data:
Toomey, Jeanne, 1921-
    Murder in the Hamptons / Jeanne Toomey.
        p. cm.
    ISBN 0-86534-223-7 : $8.95
    I.Title.
PS3570 . O56M87 1994
813' .54—dc20   94-15036
                        CIP

Published by SUNSTONE PRESS
               Post Office Box 2321
               Santa Fe, NM 87504-2321 / USA
               (505) 988-4418 / orders only (800) 243-5644
               FAX (505) 988-1025

For my family:

Sheila Terranova Beasley, Dr. Brian J. Beasley;
my son, Peter Terranova; my husband, Jim R.
Gray; and grandchildren, Siobhan, Jess and Brian
Patrick Beasley.

Cover photograph: **SOUTHAMPTON AEROSERVICE INC.**

FOREWORD

In the years since the setting of "Murder in the Hamptons," decades ago, many changes have come to society. Old barriers have been removed and people of various religions are regularly included in those gilded listings of the rich and powerful --their winter homes and their dilatory domiciles, as summer homes are separately classified. Like all of us, the chronicles of what is known as "society" move with the times.

Thus, there is no attempt in this totally fictional tale to criticize the bibles of those who live in the favorite locations of the wealthy and well born, such towns as Southampton, Newport, Saratoga and Palm Beach.

My own first introduction to Southampton came around 1928 when a courtesy aunt, Bessie Keogh, who like my family lived in Long Beach, Long Island, took me with her in her maroon Pierce Arrow to the strip of shoreline which--although also on the Atlantic--resembled Long Beach not at all.

We stopped for tea at The Mansard, a Victorian structure. Next, Bessie led me along the beach front to what I later learned was the fenced-in enclosure of The Southampton Bathing Corporation, open only to the very blue-blooded.

Then Bessie peered through the fence while I--in my best summer dress--sadly realized that I was not going to be allowed to go swimming.

Later, I learned a reason for Bessie's conduct. She was the mistress of a well known society man, Major Philip Rhinelander, whose painting in full military attire hung over her bed at 42 W. Olive St., back home.

She was apparently trying to see his wife and daughters, though I do not think that she saw them that day.

Then, with the chauffeur Howard at the wheel, we visited Southampton's Main Street where Hildreth's has been selling furniture and sundries since 1842, the Morris Studio features pictures of the street when horses were the main transport, and the major job of police quartered in the red brick Village office is frequently to console dowagers for the loss of their diamonds.

Bessie may not have had a ring on her finger, but she sure cleaned out the jewelry stores that day.

After all, she was a practical woman!

I

A bouquet of red roses, every petal clearly defined, burst in the sky and the exhibit of fireworks at the North Sea Fire Department's annual carnival was history. Another summer season in Southampton was officially underway. I hitched a ride back to Gondola Gardens with Irma Mertlich.

The next night I went to the regular Saturday meeting of the Southampton Group of A.A. My favorite speaker, a former showgirl, was leading the meeting and my favorite man, Walt Herrick, a detective on the local police force, met me there afterwards for coffee. Though possibly only a heavy drinker, not a full-blown alcoholic like me, he doesn't drink anymore to help me stay sober, a mark of true love. I looked him over approvingly. He is around five--ten with honest steel blue eyes and thick light brown hair. That night he was wearing one of his regular uniforms, a tan covert suit (he must have 12,) a white linen shirt with an electric blue tie that brought out the blue of his eyes. The design on the tie looked like windmills, a favorite theme in the Hamptons where several still stand, including one on the campus of Southampton College of LIU, which figures later on in this story.

That Sunday, I woke up early. With a small pail of cracked corn, I went out in my nightdress to feed the mallard ducks and a gaggle of ducklings on Little Fresh Pond. The water was clear. The old swamp maple which is home to Albert, a muskrat, was reflected in the lake and it was a dreamy peaceful start to a day which was to stand out as the tragic beginning of the series of violent deaths which became known in the newspapers as the Society Murders.

As I was scattering a little corn, I heard the old cowbell which serves as our front door bell clang. A uniformed policeman from the Southampton Village Police was at the door. Officer Brzozowski was a strapping blond Polish-American whose good looks made him very popular with the millionaires on Dune Road as well as the wrong side of the railroad track types like me.

"Liz, there's been an accident. Would you come with me," he said. "You probably know the woman and the Chief thought you might be able to help us notify her relatives and that.

"Not a relative," he added quickly. I was about to run in the house and check that the kids were still sleeping, not gone for an early morning swim somewhere.

I went in to get slacks and a top on and then got into the police car with him, yelling "Morning!" to my surprised neighbors, Ann and Ray Sobotka, as we drove off.

Gondola Gardens is like a tiny fiefdom. Everyone has lived there for generations and it's a safe community. Before we left the Gardens, I had waved to John O'Brien, a tall, rugged construction boss and like me the only other Mick; Mary Roessle, whose father, Robert, has long headed our Little Fresh Pond Association, and Fred Hauquitz whose son makes the best cheese cake on the Island, Wholly Moses!

As we pulled out of the Gardens onto North Sea Road, I saw Janet Marshak and Gertrude Schwed making their rounds arm in arm. The two dear ladies regularly made the circle a few times like travelers to Europe making several turns around a deck --in the old days when people still went to Europe by ship. We all know each other. During my drinking days, I think they thought of us as those crazy Irish down by the pond. Today I guess we're accepted as pretty much like everyone else. I'm a vegetarian and active in all the efforts to save Little Fresh from pollution. We now have dry wells so road runoff doesn't get into our jewel, the best kept secret in Southampton, according to a former Supervisor.

The police car headed south towards the ocean, passing Agawam Lake, which although more fashionably located, isn't half as pure as Little Fresh, I was thinking complacently. Then, I turned to the handsome cop.

"Someone drowned?"

"We don't know and I don't know the lady," he answered. "But you know her, Chief thinks. The maid said you might be able to call her relatives. She doesn't have any numbers for them."

As a former reporter for the local weekly, *The Southampton Press*, and a longtime resident, I knew almost everyone who had lived in Southampton for any length of time.

"Has she been identified?'

"Yeah, I guess. I don't know who she is. But she lives in one of those big houses on Dune Road. She's lying in front of her own house."

When we arrived, he parked the car while I went though the soft white sugar sand and there found, crumpled up on the beach, one of my few real friends among the social set, Emily Cosgrove.

"Buffy,' as she was called by her intimates, had been a good friend, very social, but generous, kind, unaffected and real --old money as Bob Gardiner would say --living by a noblesse oblige philosophy.

Walt had gotten there ahead of me. And there was a circle of uniformed police, and a police photographer, all set up and taking photographs of the scene.

"She apparently went in for a late night swim," Walt told me. I said nothing, but decided she must have been drunk. No one swam at night with Southampton's treacherous rip tide otherwise.

Dr. Emma Bellows, the medical examiner, knelt beside the body. "Dead since the early hours of the morning," she observed.

"Mrs. Grady."

It was the voice of Phil Walker, chief of the Southampton Village Police Department. I felt his hand on my forearm, gently urging me to turn around.

"Mrs. Grady," he insisted again. "Liz, please."

I saw Phil smiling at me kindly and realized with embarrassment that my cheeks were wet. There was a handkerchief in my purse, I knew, but if I reached in to get it I would see the seaweed again.

I took a deep breath and opened my bag. The seaweed was at my feet. A long strand of it stretched out along the wet sand to wrap itself around the body of Emily Cosgrove.

That must have been one of the few times seeing a dead body has bothered me. As a longtime reporter for the *Associated Press* and other news agencies, I've seen a lot of corpses. But --when you know and like someone, it hits home. Buffy was lying on her left side with her back to me, but I could still tell it was her. A few locks of her strawberry blonde hair—only slightly frosted with gray—hung from beneath the cerise bathing cap she customarily wore with her white bathing suit, because it showed off a spectacular tan. I once kidded her that she looked like a red-crested woodpecker.

"What happened?" I finally managed.

"Near as we can tell," said Phil, "she went out swimming last night. Seems she hit her head, perhaps on a jetty accidentally. Drowned afterwards looks like."

"Chief, Buffy was a celebrated swimmer. She was next to Eleanor Holm in the backstroke. She was in the Georgia Coleman class as a diver.

"If she wasn't born rich, she probably would have made it to the Olympics. She didn't have that pressure to compete!"

"Maybe in her day."

"She wasn't that old," I defended, suddenly angry at the chief's attitude. "Anyway, she's lived here all her life, and these are familiar waters. "She's saved people out here from drowning. She was a champion!"

"What are you implying, Liz?"

"I'm not implying anything." Kneeling down next to the still form, I carefully examined the back of her head. Foamy waves sloshed over my bare feet and soaked the cuffs of my slacks. "I could see where some blood had seeped out from under the cap and clotted in her hair, but most of the damage was concealed by latex.

"How long do you think she's been out here?"

Phil shrugged, "All night."

"So she went swimming last night and nobody missed her at her house until this morning?"

"Liz," Phil cleared his throat, "you know how she was."

That was true. Buffy, lonely despite her wealth, had a reputation for taking home a string of casual lovers, but then whatever appointment she'd made had most likely been missed. For what? A swimming excursion?

Having noticed nothing else unusual, I turned to Phil. "This doesn't make any sense, Chief."

"It doesn't to me, either, Liz. What do you suppose could've happened, then?"

A large, usually jolly Irish-American with black hair and gentian blue eyes, Chief Walker was the widows' delight --able to listen to their stories, compliment them on their Chanel outfits, and make an extra man at parties, a conversation piece. For in uniform --as he was now --he was a stunning man with the athletic form and broad shoulders to wear a uniform well.

Like a police dog, I seem attracted to men in uniform. I was married for ten years to a cop and was now dating another. "This is tough for you," Walker acknowledged. "Buffy Cosgrove was your friend. But that's why you might be able to help us. You know a lot about her and her family.

There were suddenly more investigators and officers surrounding the scene than there had been just a few moments before, and I realized that Phil must have been holding most of them off until he signaled them. How had I missed that signal? An officer was pushing stakes into the ground while another man looped yellow tape around each post until Phil and I were closed in on three sides.

"Who else has been this close to the body?" I asked. My voice was still shaky, and sounded like a croak.

"Just the Cosgrove's maid. She discovered her. Detective O'Neill's questioning her right now."

"Did she notice or find anything?"

Phil made a backing-off gesture with one hand. "Take it easy, Liz. We don't know yet."

"Well, if it was murder, there should be some kind of clue on this beach—footprints, something."

Phil shook his head. "We've already been up and down this stretch of sand. There's nothing. Whoever did this probably walked below the high tide line and his tracks have long since been washed away."

"There's another possibility, of course."

"Which is?"

"The murderer came by boat." I looked out at the Atlantic. Not too far offshore, I noticed a police vessel that was towing a red speedboat. "Whose boat is that, Chief? Do you know?"

Phil followed my gaze. "That's what led us to find the murder victim. Someone called the station saying that they'd seen a boat heading out to sea with nobody on board. By the time we caught up with it, it was almost six miles out. We backtracked its route, not finding anything until we reached this shoreline. The registration says it belonged to the victim." The chief looked back at me and said, "You're beginning to sound as if you're interested in this case, Liz. So, how about it?"

"Well," I hesitated, "I'm a private investigator, Phil. Nobody's hired me yet."

"Don't worry about that. You'll be getting a call soon from Higgins, Forsythe and Foster."

"Who or what is that?"

"Lawyers for the Cosgrove's insurance firm. There's probably a big policy involved here. They called me earlier, wondering whether they should contact you."

"How diplomatic of them."

Phil ignored me. "You still haven't answered my question."

Pondering my bills, stuffed in an airline envelope over my desk, I nodded. And then left with a wave, unable to say any more.

Out on Dune Road, Walt waited in an unmarked car.

"Are you okay?" he asked.

"Let's just drive around for a while," I suggested. "I want to give myself a little time to think. I can't get over realizing that someone hated her enough to kill her.

"Murder? Is that what the Chief said? When he called he just said there'd been an accident."

"No, Buffy was killed. Somebody bludgeoned her and she either drowned afterwards or died from the blows."

Walt was watching me intently, and I avoided his attentions by looking out my window. Out on the water, the police boat chugged eastward. It would have to go around Montauk Point and back to Sag Harbor, where the local police held onto vessels involved in smuggling or other criminal investigations. Maybe the police were searching for a possible lead like an unregistered boat. I thought, though, that there aren't many clues to be found in the rough waters of the Atlantic Ocean.

"Her insurance company's law firm want me to help out because I know the local scene. Saves them from sending an investigator out here."

"Could be a dangerous situation!" was all he said. But, after being around someone for a while, you begin to learn the signals, even if you don't live with them all the time. He was worried.

Walt Herrick was a detective in Sag Harbor, where he lived in a bachelor-sized Cape Cod. The location was perfect for both of us, close enough so that we could see each other

15

often, but not so close as to make it burdensome. He reminded me of the old-time screen actor, Ralph Bellamy. He had the same urbane manner, cowlick, tender smile. Now and then I admitted to myself I loved him. But I didn't want to do anything about it, like committing matrimony once again.

"All right," he said. "If anyone knew her ways and friends, it's you."

I sighed and noticed my purse was still open, so I snapped it shut. We stopped talking and he just drove around passing the Ladd house, once owned by Grover Cleveland Bacon of the presidential family; Cobble Court, where my father used to visit Wilfred Funk of Funk & Wagnall's Dictionary and then around the Murray compound.

I remembered going to A.A. meetings with Jake Murray, author of "The Devil Walks on Water," an uncanny title since he drowned, washing up on Staten Island, after a disastrous descent into pathological drinking . A derelict may have pushed him into the waters off the Battery or he might have been a suicide. His brother, Tom, had a heart attack out in the ocean and reportedly actually drowned on the beach because no one knew how to administer artificial resuscitation. Both dead by water.

How many bright stars had flared out along this stretch of priceless beach, I thought. Almost as though a doom hung over those who occupied these showplaces. Decades later, Roy Radin, the young producer murdered outside of Los Angeles over cocaine and a movie, "The Cotton Club," and Woody Allen with his ugly custody fight, right on the heels of an IRS probe over deductions he took on the house once owned by Ambassador Gerard Smith.

Whoever said that there's a broken heart for every light on Broadway might have added that there's a broken heart, too, for every grain of sand on Dune Road.

Breaking out of my reverie, I turned to Walt and asked him to drive me back to Buffy's. I had better get working if I expected to collect substantial fees and God knows I needed the money. The Cosgrove home was situated on a rise surveying the Atlantic. It was a French chateau, built by Buffy's grandfather, known throughout Victorian New York as "the Copper King." He had made his millions through smart investments in the copper fields of McGill and Ely in Nevada, where much of the family fortune still multiplied. Since the days of their great patriarch, however, the Cosgrove heirs had diversified their interests, most recently in companies involved in semiconductor research. But copper was what the family was known for, and so the Cosgrove mansion was fondly named Copper Kettles, after the manner in which the wealthy Hamptons families bestowed appellations upon their residences, such as Ocean Castle and Cobble Court.

Copper Kettles was closed off from the public by typical Southampton hedges, more than six feet high for privacy, surrounding a spectacular garden. Hundreds of rose bushes and climbers, filled the air with fragrance. Buffy, I reflected as we drove toward the house, had been very fond of her roses. She especially liked the white ones: Anastasias, Pascalis, and even the yellow-tinged Polarsterns.

A Southampton police car was parked on the circular driveway. As we walked up to the entrance, one of the massive double doors opened and Southampton Village Detective Mike O'Neill stopped himself short of the threshold. He had the choleric look I associate with some cops who take themselves very seriously.

"What're the two of you doing here?" he said.

"I've been asked to help with the investigation," I said. "Walt's just here to give me some moral support."

"It's not exactly your jurisdiction, Detective Herrick."

Walt proffered one of his resistance-withering smiles. "Don't worry, I'm not here to get in the way."

O'Neill seemed unaffected by Walt's charm. "Good. You're better off." He turned back to me. "We might need to call in the state police on this."

"Why?" I asked. "What have you learned?"

"You can come down to the station tomorrow and read the report, if you want. Right now, I've got other things in my schedule." He shoved his way between me and Walt and walked rapidly to his patrol car.

"Nice fellow," I remarked as the car pulled away.

"Sounds more uneasy to me," said Walt. "Like he's in over his head."

Anne, one of the Cosgrove's four maids, appeared in the doorway. The skin under her eyes was red and puffy. "May I help you, Ma'am?" she said, "Sir?"

Anne knew both of us from our many visits

"I know you've already been answering a lot of questions, Anne, but would you mind if we took a little more of your time?"

"You're working for the police, Mrs. Grady?"

"No, for the law firm retained by the Cosgrove's insurance company actually. Is there anyone else at home?"

"Nobody but the staff, Ma'am. Oh, and Mr. Chapelle is here as well."

"Mr. Chapelle?" Rafael Chapelle was Buffy's estranged husband, a typical lounge lizard as our forbears would describe him, a parasite in my opinion, the type so many rich women seem to have a genius for finding and marrying. He had been quite the playboy at the time of their marriage—her second—but then Buffy's romances were often reported in the columns. She might be called "the madcap heiress" or similar cliche.

Over the years, he had gradually transformed himself from playboy to aging dandy, giving up gold-plated chains around his neck for a single gold watch chain that dangled from his vest pocket.

Most of their marriage had been spent on opposite coasts, with him living in Los Angeles and her staying on the East Coast.

"Absence makes the marriage last longer!" Buffy used to argue. And I suppose, in this case, she was right. She and Rafael had stayed together a surprising number of years, though she had always kept her maiden name.

Anne invited us in, but I stopped once we were in the foyer.

"How did Mr. Chapelle get here so soon?" I asked.

"Oh, he's been here since last weekend, ma'am. Visiting Mrs. Cosgrove."

Walt said, "Is that so?"

"He's in the atrium if you'd like me to tell him you're here."

I said, "No, not yet. Could I ask you some questions first, Anne?"

Anne was one of the locals who stayed with one rich family because the lifestyle fascinated her. As the years passed, she had adopted some of Buffy's ways, enjoying a degree of fame when she crossed the railroad tracks because of her tales of the rich and famous.

"Well, you certainly can if you like, Mrs. Grady, but I've already told the detective everything I know. Here, why don't you follow me and I'll get you something to drink." Anne led us into the Cosgrove's parlor, where the decor reminded me of a French countryside chateau. The room had a welcoming atmosphere with flowers in giant Chinese vases by French doors overlooking the incomparable Atlantic, the real star of the show in those houses lucky enough to afford a view.

"Thank you, Anne, but we really don't have time," I said. "Chief Walker told me it was you who found Buffy."

"Yes, it was."

"But she was here last night, I assume."

"Yes, she and Mr. Chapelle were here most of the day yesterday. Mrs. Cosgrove said they had some things to work out. Their discussion was getting a bit hot, I'll admit, when Mr. Hughes arrived for dinner."

Richard Hughes was a stock broker, and a good one. Not only that, but he was a close friend, as well as one of Buffy's lovers. Determining whether or not he was a former lover, however, would involve a lot of guesswork on my part. He did a lot of work for the wealthiest people in Southampton and was considered a fellow with potential.

"They were discussing money then," I said.

Money problems have always struck me as a poor reason to kill, but perhaps I hold money too cheaply and life too dear. Anne backed off this line of inquiry saying only that she heard nothing else, working upstairs in the bedrooms while the butler served.

"That would be Mr. Tinsdale, but he never eavesdrops. Serves the food and wine, and leaves," said Anne, adding enviously: "He's from England, you know."

"Then you didn't catch any of their conversation?"

"No," Anne admitted. "But Mr. Hughes left, rather in a huff, too, I'd say. Then later that night the phone rang and I answered it upstairs. It was Mr. Merritt, so I went downstairs to get Mrs. Cosgrove."

"Mr. Merritt," repeated Walt. "You mean Rhinelander Merritt, the author?"

I answered for Anne, "Yes, he wrote *Life on the South Fork* and *The Hampton Society Letters*. Local color pieces on the Hamptons, though he's only lived in the area for about ten years, and most of that time he spent holed up on his boat. What did he want, Anne?"

"He asked to speak with Mrs. Cosgrove. He said it was very urgent, so I went to Mrs. Cosgrove and interrupted her latest argument with her husband. Anyway, she spoke with Mr. Merritt on the phone downstairs a while, and then she grabbed her bathing suit and left to see him, though she told everyone she was just going for a swim to cool off." Anne added, "She took the speedboat from the bayside docks."

"She went by herself?" asked Walt, who hadn't been in Buffy's company as much as I had.

"Oh, Mrs. Cosgrove loved her boats, Mr. Herrick, and the faster the better. She took care of that boat like a baby." Anne looked suddenly despondent, "The boat's lost, too, now."

"Actually, the police have already found it, Anne," I said. This news appeared to relieve Anne somewhat. "So anyway, what did Rhinelander Merritt have to say?" I asked, realizing that this must have been what O'Neill had discovered.

"Well, I haven't the faintest, Mrs. Grady. I went back upstairs to finish my cleaning."

"Anne," I said much more sternly, "What did Merritt say to Mrs. Cosgrove?"

Anne sighed, "You know, Mrs. Grady, I'm afraid you know me too well for my own good. I didn't get off the phone in time and then couldn't hang up without a click."I listened for only a few seconds. The only thing I was able to catch was Mr. Merritt mentioning something about the Blue Book."

Both Buffy and Merritt, I thought, were probably on the committee to determine who was to be listed in the volumes which officially recognized those of what was once known as the leisured class.

"Mrs. Cosgrove never came back that night," Anne finished.

"I'm sorry you had to be the one to find her" I consoled her.

There was an awkward silence for a moment. Turning to Walt, I suggested, "Don't you think it would be best if we paid Merritt a visit next? He should be able to answer a lot of questions."

"Sure," Walt agreed.

I thought out loud, "Anne, do you think we could trouble Jason for a ride?" Jason handled boats for a number of Dune Road residents who kept some small craft on the bay side of Dune Road.

Anne nodded, "I'm sure he wouldn't mind, considering the circumstances."

Walt called the Coast Guard and soon found out that Rhinelander Merritt's boat was docked at Sag Harbor. With our definite destination in mind, Walt and I went to look for Jason.

We located the young sailor, quickly, and we were soon in the eighteen-footer, cruising out of the marina on Shinnecock Bay. Jason took the shortcut through the Shinnecock Canal into Great Peconic Bay, and from there headed toward Sag Harbor, rather than going all the way around the island as the police boat had done. Once we arrived at Sag Harbor's Long Wharf, we disembarked and walked down Long Wharf to the yacht, Morning Sun, gently swinging at anchor.

O'Neill had taken the initiative. A dark blue police vessel, marked HARBOR POLICE, was docked there, and two police cars were also parked on Long Wharf..

O'Neill had seen us coming. The detective set up a ladder over the side so that we could climb aboard the more regal vessel.

"I knew you'd be here sooner or later," O'Neill said. "I'm just glad I arrived first."

I said, "I don't mean to be trailing you, detective, but it's not such a bad thing if we both work on the case, is it? Maybe we can even compare notes later on. Where's Mr. Merritt?"

"He's in one of the cabins below, but I'm afraid he's not going to tell you much."

"Well, I've heard of Merritt's reputation. He probably really resents us interrupting his work."

"I don't think he'll be bothered by any more interruptions, Mrs. Grady. Rhinelander Merritt is dead."

▼

II

O Neill led Walt and me into one of the yacht's cabins. It looked as if a hurricane had raged inside the room. Books and papers had been strewn all about the floor, the drawer to Merritt's desk was open, and, next to an overturned chair, the author's body lay on its back, a gorgeously engraved gold letter opener with a diamond on the handle protruding from beneath his rib cage. Though somewhat short of stature, he had been a handsome man with regular features and trim figure, his head crowned by straight blonde hair.

I had only seen Merritt's face in newspapers and once on the stage at Pierson High School in Sag Harbor. There he led the drive to raise money to restore the Broken Mast monument in Oakland Cemetery, a marvelous example of mortuary sculpture dedicated to the Sons of Southampton who confronted the monsters of the deep and perished in the oceans of the world.

All these noble efforts were now over. The writer lay in a pool of coagulated blood America had lost a distinguished man of letters, one whose style in recent years, decades since his violent end, has been compared to that of the current favorite, Dominick Dunne, a shrewd observer of manners and mores.

"I know you've made all the preliminary tests. Don't let me get in the way," I said in a placating tone to O'Neill. "Nothing for me to suggest."

He accepted my conciliatory manner, smiling and remarking that the lab men wouldn't have a report for some time. The entire cabin had been dusted for fingerprints.

Walt looked at the body more closely. "Seems like whoever did this has had some previous experience. The weapon goes right under the sternum and into the heart. Merritt probably died pretty quickly."

"Yeah," O'Neill agreed. "This is a lot cleaner than what happened to Buffy Cosgrove. Both socially prominent though. There may be some connection.

By this time I was sure of it. Remembering days of walking to the beach while being covered by sand from passing limousines, I wondered whether some mentally unstable individual, bitter at the contrast between his poverty and the enormous wealth he saw around him, had just flipped and was carrying out a vendetta.

Getting back to the case, the damage and ransacking indicated a search. Asked about it, O'Neill observed,. "Well, the place was searched, there's no question about that. But who knows what Merritt kept on his boat? The man was a loner."

"What about the captain?"

"Gone to New York. He left the day before yesterday, according to the log. There's plenty of food in the fridge, and Merritt was the type who'd be perfectly happy anchored in one place for days on end."

I took a look around the cabin that served as Merritt's writing room, then toured the rest of the yacht, but the search didn't turn up anything remarkable. Thanking O'Neill for his kindness and patience with me, I decided to leave while he was still in a good mood.

Walt gave me a quick hug and headed back to the police station in back to the Sag Harbor Municipal Building, a venerable red brick confection with a wedding cake tower on top.

As I passed the gray windmill, a good copy of the real ones built by the Dominys, I saw Harbor Master Jeff Brown standing there, watching a gaggle of mute swans who had taken over the Cove.

"Jeff, you know, I'm sure, that Buffy Cosgrove and now Rhinelander Merritt have been killed. Have you seen anything different or unusual --new faces around the Morning Sun, Merritt's yacht? Buffy was a frequent visitor, I think."

A burly redhead with warm brown eyes, Jeff looked very smart in his Navy uniform with starched white shirt and a lot of gold braid.

"I saw her with a fellow from Southampton, a stockbroker last week. They had a fierce argument right on this stringpiece!"

"Richard Hughes!" "Yeah. I think that's who it was. I heard her call him 'Rick' (among other things.)

I thanked him and wandered along the street which is full of great shops and restaurants, stopping at the Express office for a chat with Victoria Gardner, the publisher, and then at the American Hotel to talk to Ted Conklin who turned an old raddled lady of the evening hotel into a showplace, without marring its historic charm.

Later, Walt reappeared and drove me to my home on Little Fresh Pond. The circle of houses where I lived, called Gondola Gardens, is precious to me because my parents moved there from Long Beach in 1948 and spent their remaining years there. Just opposite the circle of cottages is what is now called the Triple H Ranch, a bar which has gone through as many facelifts and names as Zsa Zsa Gabor, whose sister, Magda, wed to Tony Gallucci, once lived here. Tony who was big in sewer pipe was not in the register, though he was active in Cafe Society, a more informal category. But he had a large bankroll, always of interest to Jolie Gabor's girls.

During my drinking days, I was a frequent customer, when it was owned by Bud Gannon and before that, the Smith's.

Now, cold sober thanks to A.A., I rarely visited any of the local pubs.

"If you don't want my peaches, don't shake my tree," is how a burly member once described his decision to forego all the Irish pubs in the Bronx.

I still felt guilty sometimes about the old days, especially as to how it affected my late husband, my mother, and the children. But –as they say in the program –-you have to forgive yourself first before anyone else can forgive you!

So I'd come to terms with it. I stopped brooding about the past and returned to reality and the cottage.

Not only my children and mother had benefitted from my sobriety, I thought, as I fed my pets. Penn Station, my wonderful part black Lab, Seth, a brown terrier mongrel, and Saint, a small, white Sheltie mix, whom I'd found starving and shaking in a Jersey cemetery, greeted me with what I fancied were secure expressions. No need to wait half the night for my return, bombed out of my mind.

The view of Little Fresh Pond is a consoling one. I sat and watched the sunfish guarding their nests in the golden sands of the pond. The tranquil scene helped me calm down.

The last few years have been spent doing PR work for a company called Hatcher Winfield, with stints as a newspaper reporter, private investigator and even, literary agent.

If it hadn't been for the tragedies, I would have been feeling very happy and content at the moment. It was almost as idyllic as when Adam had been alive. He liked to cook like Walt, but liked even better dining out in style at luxurious restaurants. I did too, Our kids were raised in the dining room of the Overseas Press Club at 54 W. 40th St., New York. Not only was the food good, but I could charge it, no mean consideration. Now, the building houses Daytop Village, maybe not so much of a departure as it seems since many were overseas in booze at the OPC, including me.

As the sign said in my last hospital stay, ALCOHOL IS A DRUG, ALCOHOL IS A DRUG, ALCOHOL IS A DRUG. I believed it and with my sponsor's help, finally put it behind me. Since she's dead now, perhaps it's OK to break anonymity and reveal her identity, if only to say thanks. She was Renee Dorr, mother of the late producer, Roy Radin. His murder over rights to THE COTTON CLUB in Gorman, outside of Los Angeles, contributed to her early death in my opinion.

Walt joined me on the dock, watching the sunfish, still vigilantly guarding their pretty nests.

"You don't feel ready for marriage yet, do you?"

"You're such a help. But, I don't really know why I can't decide. It's just...."

"You can only give your heart away once?" Walt guessed.

"I'm still in love with Adam, or at least the memory of him," I admitted. "Somehow, it would almost be like betraying him. And I don't mean just going to bed with another man. We've already crossed that bridge...." Walt grinned, and I couldn't help smiling. "No," I continued, "it'd be more like leaving him behind and forgetting him."

"You don't have to forget him, Liz. I'd never ask you to do that. I wouldn't expect you to do that. But it's okay to move on, too. I know your daughter would agree with me."

"Oh, Sheila just wants me to get married again so I'll be distracted from worrying about her at some foreign college."

"UCLA isn't a foreign college."

"Well it ought to be. And it might be someday when it drifts off into the ocean, as we all dread."

Adam had been a police detective, too, just like Walt. Sometimes I acknowledged to myself that I would always be attracted to the type: moral, strong, a man who didn't pretend he didn't understand the difference between right and wrong. But more, I was deathly afraid of losing Walt the same way I'd lost Adam, and I was afraid the closer I got to him the more that would hurt if it ever happened.

We got up and were returning to trying to work out a list of suspects when the telephone rang. I picked it up on the kitchen extension.

"Hello?"

"Hello, Mrs. Grady?" said the voice on the other end. "This is Tom Daly calling from Higgins, Forsythe and Foster. I suppose Chief Walker mentioned to you we'd be calling."

"Yes, he did."

"Good, good. Then I don't have to explain much. We'd like to retain you to investigate the murder of our late client, Mrs. Cosgrove. Would you be willing to handle the job?"

"Yes, I'm very interested."

"And what is your fee?"

"Two hundred a day, plus any expenses."

Daly agreed to my terms without a hint of hesitation and I said I would begin charging him tomorrow. I also said I'd get in to review the facts with him the next day.

So early the next morning, I hitched a ride with Peggy Ianacone, a neighbor, into Speonk and then caught the train into New York. It was an uneventful meeting. I got a few instructions, told Daly what I'd learned and headed home.

With a retainer, I felt luxurious, so I took the parlor car back.

Half asleep with The New York Times on my lap, I came to as we pulled into Southampton.

As I started to assemble my purse and the Times, I heard a scream.

"He's dead!" a fashionably dressed skinny blond cried.

"Call the police," I told a conductor, "'and tell the engineer we will have to stay here a while."

I walked over to the source of the commotion. The woman was bending over a still form. When I got closer, I was shocked to see Count Ivan Orloff collapsed in his chair. A river of scarlet ran down his elegantly tailored suit. I knew he was a Paul Stuart client since I had seen him in the store when I was buying a tie one time for Walt.

The parlor car chair has a high back which is why I hadn't seen him earlier. I knew him from various public functions. And also he often rode the train as I did when Thomas Jefferson was busy.

I heard an ambulance siren. In a few minutes uniformed police, ambulance attendants and even a reporter entered the car.

"Liz, what's going on?" asked one of the cops, a Village Police Department man apparently. It would have taken longer for the Southampton Town police to respond. But the Village office was only a few blocks from the railroad station.

"Search me," I said. "I didn't even know he was aboard."

The indomitable Dr. Bellows who had been examining him, rose to say, "He was a bleeder. We've had him in the hospital. There's a nick in the side of his neck. Someone must have cut him without anyone noticing, including him, since it was so small and done with a very sharp instrument."

An example of the murderer's weird sense of humor if, in fact, the count had been killed and this was not an accident, I thought..

Since he had been dining out for years on his claims of Russian nobility, the killer had helped him prove the truth of his stories by showing his relationship to the doomed Russian royal family. He, too, was a hemophiliac

"He's not dead!". Dr. Bellows suddenly announced. "I'll get him into the hospital, and with a few transfusions, he'll be as good as new."

"False alarm," I called cheerfully to a journalist friend, Debbie Tuma of the *Sag Harbor Express,* later the *New York Daily News* and the *East Hampton Independent.* So the murderer had failed. Unless it was just an accident--someone going by who accidentally brushed against him with a pin or manicure scissors sticking out of a purse.

I looked around the chair and spotted a fancy men's stickpin with a diamond as its focal point.

"Look at this. He may have done it to himself, reaching for something," I said.

And that was what it turned out to be — one case when the police were able to fold their notebooks with a notation -- accidental injury.

Back at Gondola Gardens, I called Walt and arranged to visit the dapper widower, Rafael, next day.

Anne greeted Walt and me at the door again and told us that Rafael would again be found in the atrium.

The Cosgrove atrium had been built in Victorian times. The glass walls, where not obscured by the exotic and endemic flora, afforded a spectacular view of the wild Atlantic --rough today with enormous whitecaps.

As I always did when I visited this room, I admired the antique wrought iron work that had been used to frame the glass panels, and the pale pink Venetian tiles that were almost too beautiful to walk on. A pair of antique Duncan Phyfe armchairs guarded the entrance. Across the room, Rafael was watering a pot filled with tall, blue larkspurs and did not seem aware of our presence. He had put on a considerable amount of weight since I'd last seen him, and his gray Brooks Brothers three-piece suit gaped at the waist. Anne beat a hasty retreat without even announcing us.

I was about to clear my throat when the recent widower said, "Do you know what kind of plant this is, Liz?"

"Looks to be larkspur," I said. It was always best to indulge Rafael, at least a little.

"*Delphinium elatum*, to be precise, but very good on your part, dear lady." Rafael put the pot and water can down and considered the flower. "It normally doesn't bloom quite this early, but you're familiar with Man's friendly taunts at Gaia. Tch, the way my wife abused these plants, I'm surprised any of them survived at all. You're Detective Herrick, are you not, sir?"

"That's right," said Walt. "I must say I'm impressed. I think we've only met once or twice before, and that was a long time ago."

"Don't be too impressed, Mr. Herrick. Who else would you be?"

Rafael went on, "At any rate, I think I'll cut this interview short by telling you all I know immediately. I had dinner last night with my wife, and during our dinner we discussed some business with our broker. What that business was," Rafael snickered at his own sense of humor, "is none of your business. Then Hughes left, we had our nightly fight, Buffy got that phone call and sailed into the night; I went to bed; the next morning my wife lay dead. You see? That's almost poetry. Shall I teach you something about horticulture now? Perhaps you're more educable than my wife was."

"Maybe some other time, Rafael," I said. "Are you sure you don't remember anything particularly unusual about last night? Did anything happen after Buffy left, maybe?"

"I was asleep, sadly alone," he said with a devilish air. "But rest at my age has taken the place of those wild nights. Poor Buffy was still a night owl." He had the grace to look suitably grieved.

Getting down to business, I observed abruptly, "You do realize, Rafael, that your alibi's not a very good one."

I can see that I'm living in a glass house," he smiled, gesturing at the atrium walls, "but it would not have been in my best interest to murder Buffy. According to her will, everything she had goes to several different trusts earmarked for her favorite charities, and I was never one of those, though I might be considered a case for charity." He plucked a flower from a nearby plant. "*Catharanthus roseus* anyone?"

I took the small, pink flower with a show of gratefulness. "Thank you, Rafael. We won't take up any more of your time."

Walt and I bowed out and went back downstairs, where Anne was still waiting for us in the foyer.

"Doesn't seem terribly upset about his wife's death," Walt commented under his breath.

"Shh. Wait 'til we're out of the house."

When we were at the door again, I said to Anne, "Tell me, Anne, did Detective O'Neill request that Mr. Chapelle remain at Copper Kettles long?"

"I should say it was more like ordered him to stay, ma'am," Anne acknowledged. "Honestly, I can't think of what I did to deserve it!"

Apparently, she meant being in charge of Chapelle.

"You didn't question Chapelle very hard," Walt observed when we had gotten back into the car.

"I don't think he did it, Walt. Like he said, he had nothing to gain from Buffy's death."

"What about jealousy then? She and Merritt could have been having an affair."

"He was gay. They really were only friends and both served on the same committees. "

"Shouldn't Rafael be worried that his allowance will be cut off?"

I shrugged. "Maybe it hasn't sunk in yet, or maybe he actually put away some of his money for a rainy day. I don't know. Anyway, the next stop is Richard Hughes' office."

"Okay." Walt glanced at his watch as he changed course, and I realized I had been monopolizing his time.

I said, "You probably have to get back to the Harbor, don't you?"

"No, no, this is more important than paperwork at my office. Besides, you know me, I'm not the workaholic you are."

"True, but I should concentrate and work on this alone, at least for the start of the case."

"What's that supposed to mean?" Walt snapped.

Sorry. Guess I'm a little tense," he went on. "Sure you wouldn't like me to come along?"

"I can handle it, Walt. I'm going to see a stock broker, not Charles Manson. Anyway, you're off tomorrow. I'd love you to come with me then. Don't alienate the Chief!"

Walt shrugged, smiled --he has a cheerful nature, sanguine, not choleric, like most cops I've known, and we drove back to Little Fresh Pond.

We stopped at Otto's Nord See Market --catering especially to the German population of Big Fresh Pond, diagonally across North Sea Road from Little Fresh –both kettle ponds left by the glacier.

I stocked up on Otto's homemade salad and strudel, and we returned to the cottage.

I looked through my mail and then called Richard Hughes's office in downtown Southampton.

"I'm glad you called," he politely began.

"I wasn't sure you'd be in, Rick," I said.

"I know. The police left just a half hour ago. They'll probably be calling on me again." I heard Rick clear his voice on the other end. "I'm, really sorry to hear about Buffy. It's the most bizarre thing I've ever heard. I mean, who'd want to do that to her? It just doesn't make any sense. And Rhinelander Merritt, too! Do you think there could be a connection?"

"That's what I'm trying to find out, Rick."

"Didn't you get out of being a lady sleuth?"

"I've decided to take it up again."

"Oh. Oh, yes, of course. Is there anything I can do?"

"May I come over and talk to you a while in your office? I'd like to hear about your dinner with Buffy and Rafael last night."

"Sure. Come on over. About how soon do you think you'll be?"

"I'll be there in about 15 minutes."

I don't drive so I called Thomas Jefferson, my favorite livery car driver since in Southampton cabs were often called something else and destinations often called "the estate" no matter what the address.

We went past the Auto Museum, Herb McCarthy's Bowden Square with his ceremonial dog house out in front, and the red brick building which was then the Town Hall, now Saks Fifth Avenue.

He dropped me off by Hughes's office. The brass plaque mounted on the stone read "Hughes & Associates, est. 1922." The firm had remained relatively small despite the kind of clientele it served. Rick had a partner whom I'd never had a chance to meet, his younger brother Dabney Hughes. The receptionist, like me, was a loyal member of the Wilderness Society, the Sierra Club and the National Audubon Society, and we had become friendly over the years.

"Hello, Liz," she greeted me cheerfully but professionally. "How are the mallards and swans of Little Fresh Pond?"

"Doing swimmingly," I quipped weakly. "Tell me, Cindy, how's he handling it?"

Cindy lowered her voice, "Well, he puts up a very good front, Liz, but he doesn't need this to add to his troubles."

"Troubles?" I asked, matching her whisper.

"The firm's not been doing well lately, I hear. Lucky for me this is a second income and my Bill can support us both."

"That bad, is it? I hadn't heard anything about this before. Thanks, Cindy. Let's talk some more later."

I entered the door to Rick's office. He was sitting behind an oversized, antique oak desk that fit him like a well-tailored suit. He was a man who was more comfortable with his possessions than with himself, always appearing to be more at ease when he was behind his office furniture or the wheel of his MG. Over the years, he had managed to gain the trust and investments of many of the socially prominent; i.e., richest families in the Hamptons, and I had assumed his financial picture was bright. Now --with Cindy's comment --I wondered if he had taken too much risk. I hoped he hadn't gotten into embezzlement, fraudulent claims, extortion or obstruction of justice, charges very familiar to many Dune Road newcomers who have tried to match the inherited wealth of their neighbors by emulating F. Scott Fitzgerald's Gatsby.

I speculated about my chances of seeing his bank account and made a mental note to check with Chief Walker on whether any claims of fiduciary mismanagement had been received.

"Hey, Liz," Rick welcomed me as I walked into the office. He had a faint but noticeably French way of enunciating his words, the result, he once told me, of spending years in Montreal. It seemed an affectation. Rick was lean and athletic for his age, which was somewhere in the mid-fifties, A health nut, he was always very careful with his diet, which had endeared him to Walt. He kept a small bowl of apples and bananas on his desk.

He was wearing a light plaid jacket, beige trousers and a white shirt. with a vari-colored ascot at the throat. He looked very smart and could have posed as the male model for The Southampton Look as my daughter, Sheila, used to do with her picture appearing weekly in The Southampton Press as the feminine model.

"How are you doing?" he asked with some concern in his voice.

"I'm fine, Rick, thank you. I'd be a lot better, though, if I could find out exactly what happened to Buffy.

"She had no enemies that I know of," he said. "I can't understand any of this. It's crazy --makes no sense."
He shrugged, then said, "I think it's great of you to help out Buffy's family."

"I'm really not too concerned about her family. I just want to see that Buffy's murderer doesn't get away with what he's done."

Rick grabbed an apple and offered me one, which I declined.

"What about Rhinelander Merritt? No one has expressed much grief. Didn't he have any close friends?"

"Well, nobody around here knows a great deal about the man. I suppose he must have family somewhere. The police will contact them, I'm sure."

"Did you ever read any of his books?"

"No. I live in the Hamptons. Why would I need to read about life here? You were with Buffy last night. You knew her well. Weren't you having a romance?" I asked, finally getting down to business.

"I was one of her retinue," Rick replied, flushing a bit. "I did care about her though, you know. She was always a good sport and a lot of fun. I was her escort at many parties here and in Palm Beach. I've got two theories so far. Number one: Buffy and Merritt might have been having an affair and one of her other lovers found out about it and put an end to them both. This isn't too implausible, I figure, since she had beaucoup beaux. Number two: Buffy's husband finally went totally crazy, and killed them both for some unknown reason --maybe to do with money."

"Well, I don't think Rafael's murderously insane, and he didn't have anything to gain from either Buffy's or Merritt's death. As for Merritt, he was gay. Surely you knew that?'

"I heard he swung both ways!"

"How about you, Rick. How were things between you and Buffy?"

"You knew her, Liz. Ours was a kind of on-again, off-again affair. You don't suspect me of killing them, do you?"

"No," I said with more conviction than I felt.

"Anything interesting come up at that last meeting?"

"Pretty dull stuff. I had to go over there to help them with a tax problem. It's not my specialty, but I do have the degree and they didn't want to go to just any accountant."

"What sort of tax problem'?"

"It seems," said Rick, tossing the apple core in his waste basket, "that Rafael had been earning some money in California without reporting any of it."

"Rafael? He's a sponger. What could he do to get a paycheck?"

"No, Liz, you don't understand. It wasn't the kind of occupation you get a paycheck for, but Mr. Chapelle was stupid enough to put some dubious earnings, his con man gains maybe, into his and Buffy's joint account, an account that was earning plenty of taxable interest. I imagine Buffy thought she had closed it out. She knew him for a leech. Probably never worried about his putting money IN." Rick paused. "You realize I'm telling you this in strict confidence because I know you can be trusted and you're trying to find out who killed her."

"You mean, you didn't tell the police anything about why you were there?"

"I kept it short. I told them I was counseling them on some stock options; that seemed to satisfy them - for now. "If I'm asked to testify, I'll tell all."

"I appreciate your candor," I said. "And, *quid pro quo*, I'll let you in on my thoughts: Both Buffy and Merritt were on the committee to determine who was going to be in the *Register.* Isn't that an interesting connection?"

"I knew Buffy was, naturally, but not Merritt. I'm kind of out of all that. Wait! I just remembered. Buffy mentioned to me once that they had hired Merritt to do some research for them on family backgrounds. It seemed a bit odd to me that they would hire a best-selling novelist to do that, but now it makes perfect sense if he was also on the committee. And, of course, he's listed in the *Social Register,* since he comes from a long line of land barons in Oregon. Do you think he might have found something to damage someone's reputation?"

"It could be," I said. "Merritt's cabin was ransacked by the murderer, who was obviously looking for something. But that wouldn't explain Buffy's death."

Rick threw up his hands in resignation, "Okay, I'll admit I'm not a super-sleuth. Frankly, the whole thing is beginning to give me a headache." He covered his face with his hands and rubbed his temples with his index fingers.

I smiled understandingly. "Me too. How about this, then? Let's take a break and I'll take you out to dinner. My treat."

"Dinner? "But , it's only 4:30."

"Yes, the perfect time to eat out before the restaurants get too crowded. Come on, I'll take you to the Drivers Seat. It's nearby, informal and the service is fast.

And, even better, I'll put it on my expense account."

Rick eventually relented, and we decided to walk to the restaurant, which was on Jobs Lane, a nearby street that had some exclusive and expensive dress shops and the Parrish Art Museum. The Drivers Seat was perfect for two people sharing a friendly meal. The waitress, wearing a crisply starched apron over her navy blue skirt and blue-and-white-striped blouse, recognized me as a regular customer and promptly led us to a corner table. Rick ordered a Guiness stout and I ordered a regular cola - I have an aversion to anything with the first name "diet."

"So how are you and Walt?" asked Rick as he adjusted himself.

I guess I looked annoyed.

"I'm sorry," he apologized,

"I know how much you like to keep your private life private. Forgive me."

We were mulling over the menu when I saw that my companion was staring across the room at someone.

"What's the matter?" I asked. "See someone?"

"Yes," Rick said absent-mindedly. "If you'll excuse me for just a minute, I'll be right back, Liz!"

"Sure," I said, bemused.

Rick got up and walked over to a man I saw seated on the far end of the bar. I vaguely recognized him, but I wasn't quite sure who it was. Rick sat down on a stool next to the man and almost immediately began to argue with him. Over the buzzing conversations from the tables around me and the clatter of plates and silverware, I couldn't make out what was being said, but Rick was talking loudly enough that I could tell the tone was anything but friendly. The other man began to yell back suddenly and then he stood up. Rick stood up, too, and grabbed the man by his lapels. The two men were now beginning to draw the attention of the surrounding patrons, and I was about to get up myself to see if I should try to intervene when the other man pushed Rick's arms aside and decked him with a right cross to the chin. Rick fell backward over a stool and several people cried out in alarm. A waitress dropped her tray and plates and glasses crashed on the floor. I ran over to Rick, and when I got there the other man was gone.

I kneeled down next to Rick, who was holding his chin with one hand and moving his jaw as if to check whether anything was broken.

"Rick," I said, helping him up, "are you okay? Who was that?"

"That," said Rick, his voice thick with anger, "was my dear brother Dabney."

▼

III

T he owner of the restaurant wanted to call the police, but I managed to smooth the situation over by explaining that the brawl had been a brief misunderstanding only and that it was certain not to happen again. Just the same, it was strongly suggested to us that we follow Dabney's example and leave the premises at once.

When Rick and I were once more on the sidewalk of Job's Lane, I asked him if he wanted to go to the Emergency Room.

"It's not that serious," he said.

"OK, but would you mind telling me what that all was back there?"

"No offense, Liz, but this doesn't involve you or your investigation." Rick touched his jaw experimentally. "I think I'll just go back to the office, get into my car, and go home."

We walked on in silence past the equally silent statues that were posed beside the Parrish Museum. The white stone figures of antiquity regarded us impassively, secure in the knowledge that they represented an ideal beauty for humanity that could be admired but never attained by us mortals. Though divinely serene and exquisitely sculpted, they could not equal in setting the gods and goddesses of mythology which adorn an avenue of evergreen arbor vitae trees in back of the Robert David Lion Gardiner mansion on Main Street, Easthampton. Perhaps the setting is not vast enough to give the feeling of immortality--of Leda, Mercury, Diana, Pan, Jupiter and--patron saint of Southampton logically, if not in fact: Neptune, posing with their symbols--the swan with Leda, Neptune with his trident, Bacchus with his grapes.

Musing about Gardiners Island and the struggle the 16th Proprietor has made to insure its protection--after his death-- from development, I was suddenly returned to the present-- back at Hughes & Associates. We parted company with a brief goodby, and I called T.J. for transportation home. I asked Thomas Jefferson to just drive around for a while.

I thought that perhaps I could go back to the Hughes office then and if Rick was gone, try to pump Cindy for more gossip, but I decided I'd had enough for one day. I could call Cindy at her home and meet her outside of the office some other time.

Satisfied that this was the wisest course of action, I got T.J. to take me home. I lay down for a few seconds, and fell asleep. The answering machine buzzed. I picked up and a familiar voice said, "Hi, Liz. It's Walt. Sorry, but I'm going to have to break our date tonight. There was more work waiting for me than I'd thought.

"Because Merritt was murdered in the Harbor here, the case has come under our jurisdiction as well, and the Chief picked me to look into it. Hey, guess that makes us a professional team, now. Anyway, I'll call you tomorrow, OK?" The next message was from Melinda Darlington. "I heard you'd been retained to work on this Cosgrove tragedy. Please call me, won't you? The number is 283-9735. It's unlisted, so I'll trust you not to pass it around. Goodbye."

Melinda Darlington? What could she possibly want? The Darlington's lived in the mansion next door to Copper Kettles.

No sense puzzling over it. I dialed the number Mrs. Darlington had given and waited for the line to be picked up at the other end.

"Darlington residence," said a stiff, male voice.

"Yes, may I speak with Mrs. Darlington, please? This is Liz Grady calling."

"Mrs. Darlington is unavailable at the moment. Would you care to leave a message?"

The butler, or whoever it was, was obviously on call-screening duty tonight.

"I'm returning her call and I'm in a bit of a rush. Would you please see if she can come to the phone? I'll hold."

There was an indignant pause. "Very well, madam," the voice replied, and I heard a clatter as he put the receiver down. At least I didn't have to listen to Muzac. I could, however, make out the sounds of people talking and laughing in the distance.

About a minute later, Mrs. Darlington picked up the phone.

"Mrs. Grady! So glad you could return my call. I haven't seen you since that party at poor, dear Buffy's last summer. It is very disturbing --really awful news about Buffy, which brings me to what I was calling you about. I thought you might like to know that a police car came by about an hour ago and picked up Mr. Chapelle. I don't think they intend to return him any time soon."

"He's been arrested? Mrs. Darlington, are you certain?"

"Quite certain. One of my maids called one of Buffy's maids to confirm our suspicions. The police seemed fairly convinced that Mr. Chapelle is the perpetrator. If he is, of course, it would be no great loss. I begged her not to marry him years ago!"

"Well," I said, "thank you for taking the trouble to call me, Mrs. Darlington."

"Not at all, darling. My pleasure. I'm afraid I can't chat any more, though. I have some guests to attend to."

"Of course."

"Thank you, dear," the cultured old voice said.

I pictured Buffy where she used to sit at our butcher board kitchen table sent from Michigan when my daughter, Sheila, was living there. Buffy had been a very down-to-earth person. We had met at a fund-raiser for the Group for the South Fork.

From there, it had been a short step to friendship, and we saw each other often, with Buffy visiting my little cottage as often as I visited her mansion.

The whole day caught up with me in a second. I sat down on the couch and cried like I hadn't cried since Adam's death. In the kitchen, I heard one of the dogs knock my plate with some cottage cheese and pineapple onto the floor. The clatter was followed by several seconds of happy licking.

▼

IV

The thump of the morning paper landing on my porch woke me up early the next morning. It was still dark outside, but according to the glowing digital clock on my VCR I had been asleep for six hours, a record. A long shower and change of clothes brought me back to my old, middle-aged self, however, and I started a pot of coffee to finish the process and fed my pets. With a cup in one hand, I went out to get my *New York Daily News*. I unfolded the paper and was greeted with the headline: "SOCIAL REGISTER MURDERS!" I read through the article, which didn't tell me anything I didn't already know. The writer's slant was that both victims had been on the register committee, and it noted that the latest edition was due to come out next month.

Chief Walker gave the standard statement to the effect that there were no suspects at the moment and that evidence was still being gathered. I was worried, however, that the story was bound to cause a lot of unwarranted speculation and rumors.

The sky was brightening to a brilliant rose tinged with gold, and the birds of Little Fresh Pond were beginning to stir when Walt rang the doorbell. We were both early risers, but I was sure he was hoping to catch me still in bed. The expression on his face when I opened the door proved me right.

"Good Morning, Liz!," he said, recovering from his disappointment as quickly as possible. "Dressed already, I see. Bet you've only had coffee so far for breakfast, though."

"Still working on it" I said, noticing that he was carrying a manila folder.

"I've got Detective O'Neill's report, actually. Since our two departments are working together now, I was able to get my hands on a copy."

"What a partner!" I said and grabbed the report. I headed back toward the kitchen, and Walt followed me. It was, unfortunately, a short and disappointing read. "There's nothing useful here, Walt."

"Well, at least you know you're not behind in the game."

"It's time to do some serious digging. I think we'll start with a visit to the Darlingtons."

"Those are the people who live next to the Cosgrove home, right?"

"That's right. Melinda Darlington called me last night and told me that the police had arrested Rafael Chapelle." I summarized the phone conversation I'd had with the matriarch.

Walt said, "Funny, but I didn't hear anything about that, even though I was at the Southampton station this morning."

"Sometimes the most direct approach isn't the most obvious one. If we go to the station, we'll just get the official word about Rafael, Buffy and Merritt, but if we go to the Darlingtons', we'll get all the unofficial gossip. And you should never underestimate the power of gossip, Walt, especially when it comes to murder."

"OK, so we go to the Darlingtons'. Or, try to, anyway. Isn't it awfully difficult to visit a billionaire's home without an invitation, documents on your family history, a passport, and three letters of recommendation?"

"Certainly, but I've got an in, remember? I've been doing PR work for their textile company. I'll just say I'm doing some follow-up work or something. Don't worry, we'll get in all right."

I waited until the hour was more respectable before calling Mrs. Darlington. She was much more accessible this time.

"Mrs. Grady, darling, of course you may come over! But I'm surprised you're worried about linen advertisements when you're on this big case."

"Well, I still have my regular obligations as well, Mrs. Darlington. I shouldn't trouble you too long."

"That's quite alright. I'm having a group of friends over to play croquet," she said, pronouncing the word in the English fashion as CRO-key, "and you can certainly join us. I thought of calling it off, but I don't think Buffy would have wanted that. She was such a lively, understanding girl. I miss her already."

"May I bring a friend along, Mrs. Darlington?"

"You mean perhaps that handsome detective friend of yours? Of course, Oh, and you can call me Millie."

"Sure, Millie. We'll be over shortly."

Walt and I arrived at the Darlingtons' around noon. The mansion was an enormous pure white frame, sprawling and high with a large deck providing excellent views of the Atlantic. There were two croquet courts, the envy of all Hamptons croquet enthusiasts. The Darlington's butler greeted us at the door and led us through the house, past a staircase out of "Gone With the Wind," rooms lined with modern artworks—I recognized a Miro and two Dalis—down hallways that I though would go on forever, and out to a rear courtyard which contained the croquet courts as well as tennis courts.

This house was historic, one of the oldest along the shore. I had once visited the attic where a spy glass was mounted on a high beam. It was used as a lookout in the old days. If anything of interest was sighted along the shore –a ship in peril or a whale -the family horn was blown, a signal which the next neighbor passed on. This is how a group of neighbors was assembled and the beach soon peopled with volunteers ready for any emergency.

"Has either madame or monsieur visited the Darlington courts before?" asked our guide, fairly sure that we hadn't.

Walt and I both shook our heads.

The butler smiled with pleasure, "Then you are both in for a rare treat because the gardens are in full bloom. I always like to watch our guests' reactions." He slowly drew back the curtains, and I couldn't help but gasp. Walt said nothing, but his eyes widened. It was like peering through Alice's Looking Glass and seeing Wonderland. Mrs. Darlington had no doubt spent tens of thousands of dollars to create a magnificent topiary garden, complete with ponds, waterfalls, walking bridges, streams, and a grand gazebo made of marble that was designed like a Roman temple. The whole thing was carefully laid out to frame two perfectly manicured croquet courts, and as usual, an eight-foot-high hedge surrounded the entire garden. I could see a number of men and women on the courts, some concentrating on the game, others milling about among leafy llamas, evergreen elephants, a giraffe and two recumbent lions, backed by poppies, day lilies, phlox, and Montauk daisies. There were also a number of rose trees.

The Queen of Hearts herself appeared from behind one of the bushes.

"Oh, there you are, darling!" said Melinda Darlington. A woman in her seventies at least, she looked frail but was stylishly attired in a red-and-white print silk pant suit over which she wore a white cashmere sweater to protect herself from the sometimes chilly ocean breeze. "And Mr. Herrick, how nice to see you," she added.

"I'm delighted to be here, Mrs. Darlington," said Walt.

"Oh, please, call me Millie. How do you like my garden?"

"It's absolutely magnificent!"

"It's like a fairy land," I agreed.

Millie beamed, "I was hoping you'd say something like that. Here, let me show you something." Millie led us over to one of the rose trees and pointed to a rose that was almost completely open. "You see this one? Notice the red-and-white coloring. Can you guess the reasoning behind it?"

It dawned on me that my initial impression had been correct. I blurted, "The rose garden from *Alice in Wonderland!*"

"Exactly!" Millie laughed giddily. "You see," she pointed again at one of the blooms. "I had a horticulturist in England breed these especially for this garden. There are no others existing in the entire world with quite this vibrancy of hue, petal shape, and mix of colors that makes it look like red paint is dripping off the petals. They're called, naturally, `Alice in Wonderland.' This particular tree," she added, indicating the plant she was next to, "is my favorite. I never let anyone care for it but myself."

Suddenly, recollecting herself, she said, "You had something you wanted to discuss about my company?"

"Yes, but you know what? As we were driving over, I realized it wasn't that pressing and I could resolve it with my boss at Hatcher Winfield. It was just some details about bids from advertising firms."

"Sounds dreadfully dull, darling. Thank you for taking care of it." Millie smiled, "Well, since you're here, why don't you join the rest of the company?"

"We'd love to, thank you."

Millie led Walt and me over to where most of the activity was. Two teams of players were concentrating on their next shots while about half a dozen other guests were sitting around white, ornate iron tables,

The sky was clear but hazy, causing the light from the sun to sparkle off the slightly damp vegetation in a way that gave the impression that one was entering a pointilistic scene conceived by Seurat, an effect that was heightened by the fact that two of the women were carrying dainty shade umbrellas. There were trays displaying shrimp, crab cakes, and crackers, as well as pitchers of iced tea. An outdoor bar provided stronger drink for those who preferred it.

I recognized Millie's husband, Avery Darlington, and I could pick out some of the other guests as people I'd seen at some of Buffy's parties: Louise Witt, the young and beautiful relative of J. Pierpont Morgan whose name often cropped up in the *Southampton Press's* gossip column; Frank Stewart Campbell-Spenser—a descendant of a very distant relative to the poet Edmund Spenser, a fact he rarely failed to work into a conversation, even if you were just commenting on the piquancy of the clam dip; Mrs. Amelia Campbell-Spenser, his wife; and on the court I saw Mr. and Mrs. Edward Pierson, honored guests, no doubt, since Mr. Pierson was a descendent of a respected family that had originally settled in the Hamptons during the seventeenth century. One of the men who was standing a little way off was Colonel T. Everett Stiers, another prominent figure in social circles and a frequent party goer. I didn't know the man he was talking to, nor could I tell which of the others the Piersons were competing against.

"Ah! Mrs. Grady and Mr. Herrick," said Avery, suddenly noticing us from his seat at one of the tables, "won't you join us?" He was sitting with the Campbell-Spensers, which did not bode well, but I accepted anyway. "Frank, Amelia," Avery continued, ignoring his wife as she wandered off to talk with someone at another table, "do you know Mrs. Grady and Mr. Herrick?"

"Please, just call us Liz and Walt," I said.

Frank and Amelia greeted us kindly, and then Frank said, "I've heard that you're trying to discover who is responsible for those terrible murders."

"That's right," I admitted. "Millie told me last night that they arrested Buffy's husband." I turned to Avery, "Perhaps you or your wife could lend some insight as to what's been going on over at Copper Kettles. Assuming the police might be right, did you notice any warning signs that back up the police theory that Rafael is guilty?"

"He's never around. The man only arrived last weekend from Los Angeles. It doesn't seem like he'd have any reason to do it, especially when Buffy told Millie that she'd left nothing in her will for him and he wasn't a beneficiary of her life insurance. I know this because she used to speak very frankly about where her relationship with Rafael stood. I'm sure she's said the same to you."

"Yes. So that leaves me at square one again."

Frank cut in, "Oh, I don't think that's true at all. Didn't you see this morning's paper? This case has a very clear definition to it: both Buffy and Rhinelander were on the Blue Book committee, the members of which are at this moment selecting the people who are to be listed in its pages. Obviously, someone has been snubbed, and whoever the snub-ee is has somehow discovered this fact and is out for revenge. My guess is that the next person to be murdered will also be a member of the committee."

Walt said, "You expect there to be another murder?"

"If I'm right, there has to be," said Frank.

"It's an interesting theory," I said.

Amelia wrapped one arm around her husband and remarked, "Frank is very clever about this sort of thing. He reads a lot of mystery novels."

"All you have to do, then," concluded Frank, obviously relishing the attention, "is talk to the other people on the committee and find out who was up for consideration who didn't make the cut. Then you'll have a list of prime suspects."

"Do you know of anyone who might be on that list?" I asked.

Frank thought for a moment. "Well, there's Ary Joyant Dault. She was blackballed when she married that Jewish broker. He was unknown to society. There are some distinguished Jewish families included in every listing of our set."

"Not dear Mrs. Dault!" said Avery. "She's rather old to be stabbing people in the heart and hitting them over the head, don't you think? And besides, she was married years ago and has long since become a widow."

51

I remembered, though, that Ary Dault was a champion swimmer and still did well in senior competitions. She was certainly in better shape than most people 30 years younger. *In fact, I realized with a stab that she was actually no older than me.*

"Well, then," ventured Frank in a more conspiratorial tone, "it might be our friend Mr. Goode over there." With a slight motion of his head, he indicated the man speaking to Colonel Stiers. "He's ambitious and rich, but doesn't have the background."

Amelia scoffed, "You're just saying that because he ignored you at the Westons' party last month."

"He didn't just ignore me, dear, he embarrassed me in front of our friends."

Amelia leaned over towards me and winked, "It seems that Andy Goode remembers his lines to *The Fairy Queen* better than Frank."

"Do you have to tell everyone?" Frank snapped, then adding to Walt and me, "You miss one line to the eighth canto of the second book and they jump all over you!"

Just then, the Piersons, having finished their game, walked over to our table with the other couple. Judging by Mr. Pierson's grin, I guessed that he and his wife had defeated their opponents, who nonetheless seemed to be taking their defeat with dignity.

"Edward, I see you and your lovely wife have won again," said Avery.

"Yes, but it was no easy match by any means," said the victor. "The Viscount and his lady played brilliantly. I must say, I'm glad the weather's warmed up enough to play again and for our English friends to visit us once more."

The Viscount bowed slightly to Mr. Pierson. "I readily concede our defeat to the better team. Come dear," he said to his wife, "let's get some iced tea. I'm parched."

Pierson watched them go before wondering aloud, "Now that I've shown Albert a thing or two, who can we play next?"

"How about Andy?" suggested Amelia.

"No, no," said Frank, "he's from Westhampton. They don't use the Southampton rule book, and Edward would have to spend too much time teaching him how to play the game correctly."

Mr. Pierson sighed at his dilemma. "Perhaps it's time for a break anyway. May we join you?"

"By all means," said Avery. Our host introduced everyone, and we were all soon on a first-name basis.

"We were just discussing the story in the paper this morning," said Frank to Edward. "You know, the murders. Liz here is on the case with Walt."

"It's a horrible thing," said Edward. "Why, I've known Buffy for ages. Her parents were close friends of mine." I remembered now how whenever Buffy talked about her childhood, the Piersons had often been involved in the scenario. Buffy's parents had been killed when their plane crashed over Germany, where her father had some business interests. After that, the Piersons didn't visit Copper Kettles nearly as often. It seemed as if the Cosgrove clan was under some sort of terrible curse. Then I recalled something else about Edward Pierson.

"Edward," I posed, "if I remember correctly, you and Buffy's father were involved in some business investments together."

"Pharmaceuticals," Edward confirmed. "It wasn't too profitable, however. We were competing against Hoechst AG, which is a giant in the industry now, of course."

"Buffy's maid, Anne, told me yesterday that only hours before Buffy's death, Richard Hughes came over for dinner to discuss business with her and her husband, but she didn't know what it was all about. Apparently, the discussion turned into a serious argument."

"Really? Between whom, the Cosgroves and Hughes or Rafael and Buffy?"

"I'm not sure. Would you know if Buffy was in any financial trouble—maybe because of Rafael? Or are there perhaps any businesses the Cosgroves are involved with that are in trouble, such as their copper mining ventures? I've heard you own some stock in McGill and Ely."

Edward guffawed, "My dear lady, you're awfully forward, aren't you? Would you care to review my portfolio while we're at it?"

"I'm sorry," I apologized, "but this is a murder investigation. I need to know as much as I can."

"Of course. I understand, but if you're looking for anybody suffering from financial problems who was at that table that night, don't look at Buffy. She had an excellent good business sense for a woman, and she knew enough to keep Rafael out of her checkbook. It's Hughes who's having difficulties at the moment."

Avery looked surprised. "Is that right, Edward? You know, his brother is handling a lot of my holdings, but if they can't handle their own affairs how should I expect them to handle mine?"

"Exactly the point," said Edward, "which is why I've gone to another broker. I made the switch just last week, in fact."

"Who did you go to?"

"Weston & Taylor. Here, I'll give you their card."

"Thank you," said Avery, "I—," but our host wasn't able to finish his thought before a frightened scream from one of the other tables cut him short.

"Avery! Your wife!" It was the Viscount's voice. Everyone at Avery's table jumped out of their chairs as we looked over to see Millie Darlington slumped over the table where the Viscount was sitting. He was holding his frightened wife in his arms.

▼

V

Avery ran over to his wife's side, and Walt and I were not far behind.

"Call an ambulance!" I said to Walt after one look at Millie's pale face, and he changed course toward the house.

"Oh my God, oh my God, she's not breathing!" Avery panicked.

"Was she eating anything?" I asked the Viscount.

He shook his head, "No, she was just drinking some tea, and then her face became pale, and the next second she fainted."

"I'll do the Heimlich on her," said Avery.

"No! Stop!" I yelled at him. "Aren't you listening? She's not choking." I felt for a pulse in her wrist, but couldn't detect even a weak heartbeat. I checked her eyes, which were partially dilated, the left one more than the one on the right. "It might be a stroke, but I'm not sure," I said. "We'll have to try to get her breathing again. Avery, help me to lay her down on the ground. Gently." His hands shaking, Millie's husband helped me to ease her onto the grass and I began to administer CPR, a skill no one in my line of work should be without.

A couple of minutes later, Walt returned and said an ambulance was on the way.

"Here, Walt, you take over. I'm starting to get tired."

Moving out of Walt's way, I checked for Millie's pulse again. Still nothing. A crowd of stunned guests gathered around us. It seemed like forever before I finally heard the sound of the ambulance's siren.

Backing through the side gate to the garden, the ambulance was able to pull up within a couple of yards of where Millie lay, its way blocked by one of the topiary elephants. Two paramedics jumped out of the van, and while one retrieved the gurney from the back the other rushed to Millie's side as Walt moved out of the way.

I quickly explained to him what had happened as he examined Millie.

"OK," the paramedic said as he opened the case he brought with him. "No pulse." He took out a syringe and injected her with what I guessed to be adrenaline; then, as his partner arrived, he put an oxygen mask over Millie's face. "Come on, Hal, let's hurry it up. You drive and I'll stay in the back." They lifted Millie onto the gurney and sped her over to the back of the ambulance. In an instant, they were all in and the van was pulling away.

"I'm following them," said Avery, and he ran back into the house.

"Wait!" Frank called after him, "Amelia and I will come with you."

Walt and I remained with the other guests, unsure of what to do next.

"Should we go with them?" I asked Walt.

He shook his head, "Not right now. We'd only be in the way. We can catch them at the hospital in an hour or two. Come on, I think it's time we should be going."

I nodded. We probably couldn't be of much help right now. Our departure was a quiet one, and as we made our way back to the Darlington's back door, the crowd behind us began to buzz nervously. Several other people decided to leave as well. I guessed that in a few minutes everyone would be gone and the house would be silent, except for the sounds of the butler keeping vigil over the Darlingtons' belongings, and, of course, the Southampton Village police guarding a crime scene.

"I'll tell you, Walt," I said after we had returned to my house, "my nerves are a wreck. I'm going to call the hospital and see how Mrs. Darlington is doing."

"I guess you could do that, Liz, but you probably won't find out anything. She probably hasn't been there but a few minutes by now." Walt could tell by the look on my face that I was resolved to call anyway, so he said, "I'll fix us some herbal tea while you're at it."

Walt disappeared into the kitchen as I dialed the phone.

"Southampton Hospital," answered a woman's voice.

"Yes, I'm calling about a patient: Mrs. Melinda Darlington. She was admitted there a short time ago."

"Who's calling, please?"

"My name's Liz Grady. I'm a neighbor of hers and I promised to keep her family informed."

"Hold on, please."

There was a pause. In the background, I could hear phones ringing, doctors being paged, the general bustle of a busy hospital. The silence grew uncomfortably long.

"Um, Mrs. Grady?" came the voice at last.

"Yes?"

"I'm terribly sorry, but Mrs. Darlington was pronounced dead upon arriving at the hospital.... I'm very sorry."

"Oh, my God." I hung up the phone.

"Liz?" Walt came in from the kitchen. "What's going on?"

"Mrs. Darlington's dead. She didn't even make it to the hospital."

"Holy.... God, I don't know what to say. Poor Avery. I hope he's going to be okay."

"I don't know. Avery Darlington always treated his wife so coldly, it seemed. Practically ignored her completely at the party. But when she passed out, he seemed really worried."

"What are you getting at, Liz?"

I shrugged, "Just that it's strange how people can take each other so much for granted, I guess." I looked at Walt.

Dressed in a white polo shirt and gray slacks, his hair neatly trimmed and his face strong and kind, I could easily picture him as a fine father figure, if only it weren't so late in our lives.

"Walt," I said at last, "have I been taking you for granted?"

"Hell, Liz, I wouldn't say that. Maybe you've been kind of preoccupied lately, but that's understandable."

I shook my head, "No, I don't mean in the last couple of days — I mean the last couple of years."

Walt smiled, "If I thought that, would I be stickin' around?" He walked up to me and hugged me. Somehow he knew that's what I was asking for. "I love you, Liz, you know that." He kissed me. It was the kind of warm, sweet kiss that expresses true love. I was deeply moved..

When it was over, I said, "I love you, too, Walt, in my way." He gave me a rather wary look, but then the kettle began to whistle insistently, which brought us back to reality.

Walt cleared his throat. "I'll get that. Why don't you sit on the couch for a while and I'll bring you a cup?"

"No, I'll help. It's about time I stopped letting you do all the serving around here like you were my butler or something."

We went back into the kitchen and I poured the water while Walt added a little honey and lemon. Pouring hot water and making cheese sandwiches were about my speed. Sitting back for a few minutes rest, we went over the three personalities now on slabs at Southampton Hospital's morgue. Buffy Cosgrove, Rhinelander Merritt and Millie Darlington. Three harmless people. Outside of the society committee, what else did they have in common? Money was the only answer I could think of.

The phone rang, an annoying interruption.

"Hello," I snapped.

"Liz? I'm glad I caught you. I wasn't sure you'd be at home."

"Cindy?"

"Yes, it's me. Have you seen Mr. Hughes today?"

"No, but I'd like to see him."

"He hasn't been in all day today. I've been calling everyone, and as far as I can tell, you were the last person to see him since yesterday. Have you talked to him today by any chance?"

"No. I haven't seen him since yesterday's dinner. Is there anything wrong?"

"I don't know. It's just that he's never not come to the office unless he was sick or there was an emergency, and then he always calls to let me know."

"Well, I'll certainly call you if I hear anything. I'm sure there's a perfectly good reason why he hasn't called and by the end of the day you'll find out he's just fine."

"I hope so." Cindy's voice was concerned. "With everything that's been going on lately, I'm really beginning to worry."

"I'm sure he's fine," I reassured her again. "Don't worry. I'll see what I can do to track him down for you. No charge," I added, trying to lighten the mood and ease Cindy's tensions.

"Thanks, Liz. I'll keep looking, too. Call me if you hear anything."

"I will. I'll call you soon."

I hung up the phone and turned to Walt. "Now Richard Hughes is missing. What's going on here, Walt? All of a sudden, it seems like all of Southampton has gone berserk."

"I don't have a clue, Liz. What should we do next, do you think?"

I shrugged. "It's getting to be more than one person can track." I thought for a moment. Walt handed me my teacup, and I took a sip absentmindedly. "It looks like we're going to have to split up. I might have an idea where Richard is. Will you go to the hospital for me and see if you can find out anything more?"

"Sure. Anything I can do. Where do you think Hughes is?"

"From what I can tell, he had a pretty rough day yesterday. And if I were him, I might go somewhere to be alone for a while. You know the Montauk Lighthouse?"

"Of course I do."

"Did you also know that it was Rick and Dabney Hughes who've been spearheading its renovation? It's kind of been their pet project, in fact. I can't think of a better place for some calm reflection."

"Really? How can you be so sure that he'd go there, instead of maybe a bar or some place like that?"

I shook my head, "Richard's not the bar-hopping type. But if he's not there I've got a couple of other places in mind to check."

The strategy planned, Walt drove off to the hospital while I called Thomas Jefferson for his cab. With an expense account, I felt a little freer about taking a cab to Montauk. It was a pleasant 34-mile drive up the highway to Montauk Point, where the pyramidal lighthouse stood next to a grassy bank. Authorized for construction in 1795 by George Washington himself, the lighthouse was completed two years later at a cost of slightly over twenty thousand dollars. The "Keepers of the Light," founded by Jacob Hand not long after the beacon was completed, had maintained it for generations; and in more recent years, electricity and high-powered halogen lights had replaced the sperm oil, kerosene, and steam used to power the old lamps that had once been used.

Despite the efforts of the community and local preservationists to keep the lighthouse in use, however, the historical landmark was now threatened by an unavoidable encroaching force. The ocean had begun to erode the shoreline perilously close to where the building stood. In order to save it, sea grass had been planted around the base to help stay the encroaching sea. But this was only a temporary measure. A permanent solution is either impossible or might call for actually tearing down the historic structure and rebuilding it safely far from the fearsome brink. That's where Hughes & Associates came in. Last year, they organized some successful fund-raisers to preserve this most way-out part of Long Island from destruction.

As T.J. pulled into the adjacent parking lot, I found that my guess had been right. I recognized Rick's MG. The door to the building was locked tight, so I pounded on it as hard as I could in case Rick was on the top level. After waiting a moment, I pounded again and was rewarded with the sound of approaching footsteps. I heard a heavy bolt sliding open and Richard opened the door.

I greeted a tired looking Rick who asked with a slight frown, "How did you know I was here?" I had always thought of him as one of those good looking men who was born to lead in the community, in business, even in sports. He had a reputation as a tennis player and was a noted golfer in a town where my own dentist, Dr. Peter McGuinn once was quoted as saying that he opened a practice in Southampton because of all the golf courses, some of them quite renowned. Now, Rick seemed depressed, even glum.

In an effort to cheer him, I laughed and said, "Well, I'm a sleuth. Naturally I could find you."

He ignored my attempt at humor. "So, you've found me. What do you want?"

"Cindy's been getting really worried about you. I volunteered to help track you down."

"Well, she should have guessed where I was if she couldn't reach me at my usual haunts.

He had set up a small office for the fundraising and promotion effort. Using old furniture from the days when the lighthouse keeper made his home on the grounds, Rick had assembled a comfortable-looking rocking chair next to a reading lamp, a table that had an open book resting on it; and there was a hammock, a pot-bellied stove, and a cabinet for snacks. Richard had a portable electric heater plugged into an outlet next to the chair. In the center of all of this was a spiral staircase leading up to the revolving lamp at the top.

A couple of lonesome Coast guardsmen were his only companions at this lookout station. The light from Montauk was the first object seen by returning travelers from Europe. "Looks very cozy," I observed.

"Like it? Its my little getaway. Some people go to Europe or the Bahamas to escape life's problems; I come here. It's kind of like getting a grip on reality again after being immersed in portfolios and stock reports. Of course, when the tours start again, I'll have to move my stuff out and find someplace else. Why don't you have a seat?"

"Thanks, but there's only one chair. Where will you sit?"

"I'll just sit on the stairs here. So sit." We both sat down, and then Richard said, "You're probably wondering why I'm hiding out here like a kid in his fort in the woods."

"Well, I suppose we all need our space now and then. I heard your business was having some trouble, Rick. But I know your record—and your reputation. You'll be able to pull it into the black again."

"You're so certain?" Richard scoffed. "I wish you could convince my clients. They're starting to leave me like rats from a sinking ship."

"Why's that? I mean, if you don't mind my asking."

"We really took a beating this year."

"How would anyone find out if you made some bad investments?"

"Oh, not me, the company. Actually, my brother Dabney."

"Dabney? Is that what you two were fighting about at the Drivers Seat yesterday?"

"Sure!"He's got it in his head that he can make us billionaires by playing the market, but I keep telling him he's taking too many risks. Last week, he proved I was right by losing us—well, by losing us a lot of money. That one deal put us in the red."

"I don't get it. Why is he investing for the company instead of for himself?"

Richard shook his head, "Because he wants to prove to everyone that he can run Hughes & Associates better than I can. Dabney's always been very competitive ... and a little flaky."

"Flaky? What do you mean by that?"

Richard laughed, but I could see he was embarrassed. "You know, I have no idea why I'm telling you all this,

"Well, I won't tell anyone else if you don't want me to."

"I'd appreciate that." Richard took a deep breath. "Anyway, by flaky I mean Dabney's always behaved kind of intense since our stepfather died. He committed suicide when we were teen-agers, and it's always been pretty rough on him."

"I'm sorry." I paused, then asked, "But why should it have been any harder for him than for you? You must have been just as affected."

"Dad and I had a falling out when I was sixteen. I was eighteen and starting college when he died; Dabney was thirteen and was still in kind of the father-worship stage and never saw what a total jackass he could be. Well, don't get me wrong, I loved my stepfather, but he was as bad then as Dabney is now. He went through foreclosure. It was awful! After my stepfather's suicide, mother became very depressed; blamed herself, and eventually she had to be put into a mental hospital. Hughes & Associates was run by our uncle for a time, and then I took over just before he passed away. Naturally, I was already pretty much established in the business before Dabney was able to become a partner. So basically, Dabney resents me because I was born first and got a leg up on him. Is this getting boring for you yet?"

"Boring? No, not hardly. Does talking about it help any?"

Richard sighed, "Yeah. You know, it does some."

I smiled and got up out of the chair, comfortable as it was. "Are you ready to rejoin the real world again?"

"Is anybody? Hey, before you go let me pay you back by showing you something."

He led the way up the steep, curving metal staircase with me cautiously trailing behind. Once there, however, the climb was more than worth it. Before us, the vast Atlantic. It was late afternoon; the sun was behind us, so it was easy to appreciate the tranquil blues of the sky and ocean without much sunlight glare. A salty breeze and the cry of a distant seagull helped me to forget for a moment the events of the last couple of days.

"It's an incomparable sight," I said. "I think I see a whale spouting!"

"Thanks. I invented it," said Richard.

I laughed. "You seem to be in a better mood already."

"Thanks to you." Richard put his hand on mine and I quickly withdrew mine. "Careful," he said, "you can't lean on this railing too hard. The wood's rotten, and they haven't gotten around to replacing it yet."

"I really should be going now. You too, don't you think? Cindy's expecting you back."

"Cindy can wait," said Richard. "I'm glad you came here instead of her." He moved a little closer to me and I backed off.

"Look, Richard, don't misinterpret why I'm here."

Richard stopped short. "Oh, I understand now." He regarded me critically. "You're here because you're still considering me as a suspect in Buffy's and Merritt's deaths."

"No, that's not it at all." But since you ask, what were you arguing with Buffy about the other day at Long Wharf? I hear you had quite a battle on the stringpiece."

"Don't try me," said Richard. "I've been around long enough to know when someone's playing games with me. I think it's time you got going! What's the count? Three down and more to go?" He turned back to face the Atlantic,

I went back down the stairs and returned to Thomas Jefferson who was dozing at the wheel.

We headed back westward.

T.J. is a Southampton institution. My mother and father rode with him and now I do and my children when they're home. He's an old friend with more class, distinction, merit --whatever you call it --than half his passengers.

"T.J.", I said. "You know, I've always admired you. You put all your children through college and you worked days for the Highway Department and drove the cab nights and you're just wonderful!"

"Oh, Miz Grady. That ain't the way I did it," he interrupted. "Nice old white lady used to let me leave the alcohol on her farm. I was a bootlegger, you know. THAT'S how I saved the money for the kids' college. Sure, I did work for that department and drove the cab. But the REAL money came from selling government alcohol like your Daddy did."

He was right. During the Depression of 1929, besides running drugstores, my father, a pharmacist, had a cellar full of government alcohol which he sold on prescription to customers who were supposedly so addicted that it was considered a medical necessity. Also, it was sometimes prescribed in those innocent days as a tonic. I used to sit on top of the phone booth and call "Quelqu'un."

We both roared with laughter as the old black sedan rumbled along Old Montauk Highway passing Gurney's Inn where my son, Peter, once worked as an assistant manager, and a string of oceanfront motels. Between these commercial establishments were the great dunes. Covered with brilliant green seagrass, they faced the ocean, offering a barrier between the wild Atlantic and the road, destroyed at man's peril.

Once back home, I called Cindy up, letting her know where her boss could be found and that he apparently didn't wish to be disturbed, but at least he was safe. Going into the bathroom to freshen up a little, I found a note on the mirror. It was from Walt. It read:

Dear Liz:

Got back from hospital. Thought I'd meet you here and waited, but had to get going. Important news —

M. D. was poisoned — not a stroke or heart attack!!!
Called Southampton police and went back to D.
house. See you there?
Love,
Walt

Suddenly it hit me. Rick said three deaths!!! How had he known?

▼

VI

The Darlington home had several cars parked in front of it, none of which was elegant enough in my opinion to belong to the Darlingtons. At the door, I explained to an officer who I was and showed him my identification. He let me in, and as I made my way into the living room I ran into Phil Walker.

"I heard what happened, Chief," I said to Phil. "Have you found what killed Mrs. Darlington?"

Phil held up a bottle of pills. "Have it right here."

I looked at the label, which was homemade. "This is marked Vitamin C, Phil. What's this about?"

"It's rosehips, actually, Liz. Mrs. Darlington used to make them herself from her own roses. According to Mr. Darlington, his wife used to pop these like candy because she believed Vitamin C would prevent her from getting old –like bee therapy, Vitamin E and all the other gimmicks for staying young."

Since my late father was a chemist, I was well aware of how popular anti-aging nostrums were in Southampton. Old age was one quantity that could not be bought off though facelifts helped.

"So how'd she ...? Did someone switch pills on her?"

"I don't know. All I know is that just before she died, Mrs. Darlington excused herself from her guests to take her afternoon Vitamin C therapy. I'm sending this to the lab. If you'll excuse me, Liz."

Phil brushed passed me, and then I noticed Walt talking to Detective O'Neill. Walt looked over in my direction and waved me over.

67

"So, Mrs. Grady," said O'Neill. "Got any ideas now?"

"Sure," I said. "For starters, you've got the wrong man in jail."

"That's assuming the homicides are related. Chapelle could still have easily committed the first two."

"They're related, I'm sure."

"Oh, yeah? What makes you think so?"

"Because Millie Darlington was on the Blue Book committee, as were Buffy and Rhinelander Merritt." I turned to Walt, "Frank might have been right after all, Walt. Maybe I should hand over my license to the mystery readers."

O'Neill stared at me

"What are you talking about?"

"It's a theory I'm exploring."

"Well, explore all you want to, but theories aren't worth much unless you can prove them in court. I am beginning to see a pattern, though. The pattern is that you always arrive after the police are already on the case. You know, you're really wasting your time and your client's money."

Walt's temper flared up.

"That's a negative attitude, especially when you don't know what's going on any more than anyone else. Let's pool our ideas and suspicions and maybe we'll get somewhere." O'Neill shook his head, but then he smiled, waved and left Walt and me standing in the middle of the Darlington's living room, which was slowly emptying itself of police officers and detectives.

"Walt," I said, "you don't have to defend me. I can take care of myself!"

"I understand. He just annoyed me. The guy doesn't have a clue. Personally, if I were him I'd be grateful for all the help I could get."."

"Maybe he's right, Walt. I'm not getting any closer to this than O'Neill or Chief Walker."

"What are you talking about? Of course you are. What about Frank's idea? We know that all three victims were on the Blue Book committee, and whoever poisoned Mrs. Darlington's pills had to have been in this house within the last few hours. That makes it very likely it was one of the guests at the party. Now, if we can match someone who was a guest here today with a name of someone who was about to be rejected from the register listings, we'll have our prime suspect."

"Sounds good on the surface, Walt. But, then again, it's all so pat. Unless the murderer is a nut who doesn't mind if he gets caught, why would he be methodically drawing up a list of victim names that will inevitably point right to him?"

"Maybe he's stupid, or overconfident."

"Or maybe he's got something else in mind."

Walt looked baffled. "What?"

"We'll run it down!"

We headed up to Sal's Market where Evie Honnett, a curly headed strawberry blond then, a little gray now, with knowing gentian blue eyes, reigns over her special world of coleslaw and pickles..

All of North Sea knows that if Evie is not at her counter, she's out on the boat, SOME DAY. Her sons, Paul and John Distefano, back her up when she wants to desert the deli-cum market family business for Peconic Bay. We stocked up on vegetarian fare:: lettuce, tomatoes, celery and cucumbers and some of Evie's delicious potato salad, a morally satisfying menu for me, a vegetarian, though not a vegan. I still eat clams and shrimp, but no meat. And Walt, bless him, never complains.

"That macaroni salad was especially, good , Evie!" I called to her as we left.

Before returning home, we took a drive down North Sea Road to Peconic Bay and just watched the shore birds for a while. Robins Island, recently purchased by a billionaire, and hopefully, saved from development, loomed up out in the bay.

On the left-hand side sprawled Cow Neck Farm,, the largest farm on the South Fork, owned by Peter Salm, a grandson of Colonel Harry Huddlestone Rogers, who --with John D. Rockefeller, founded Standard Oil of New Jersey. Millicent Rogers, a noted beauty lived there in the mysterious "Port of Missing Men," right off North Sea Road, like my own minuscule holding.

All these huge estates represent the genius (or piracy) of some ancestor if they have come to the current owner by inheritance. Robert D.L. Gardiner, the 16th Proprietor of Gardiners Island, always reminds me of the fact, that behind every big garden party and estate in Southampton, East Hampton or Palm Beach, are the sweating backs of thousands of men in the steel mills of Birmingham, or somewhere else. A sobering thought.

The sky was beginning to gray into twilight already as Walt and I parked our cars in front of my house. I could hear the dogs barking with excitement at our arrival, which happened to coincide with their dinnertime.

Penn Station, Seth, and Saint practically knocked me down as we came in through the door. I went immediately to the pantry and fed them all before collapsing on the couch.

"Okay," I said, "so tomorrow we start talking to the other committee members and get a list of people who've been rejected from the listings. Sounds like it's going to be a long day. I could use a drink."

"Time for a meeting," said my geriatric beau.

"Not that kind of a drink. But I'm game. Let's go!"

He shook his head, and said, "No one can get really close to you. It's as though you freeze up when anyone tries to really know you, what you're thinking, where you are."

Walt," I said after I'd managed to control myself a little. "I shot di Bargio. But it was too late. Adam was dead, and it was my fault!"

"No it wasn't. It was di Bargio's."

"How can you be a cop and say that? You have to be responsible for your partner, and Andy was my partner that night, though in an unofficial sense. Even if he hadn't been my husband, I should have prevented his death."

He had finally wrung out of me an admission that I still felt remorse and guilt over the fatal shooting of my husband as I looked on, helpless.

Walt nodded with comprehension. "I think I understand now, Liz. I can see why you might be holding back, but let me tell you—and I think you really know this, at least intellectually—just because this happened once, doesn't mean it has to happen again. And feeling guilty and being overly cautious to the point where you're ineffective isn't going to help anyone; it's not going to stop another death, and it certainly might inhibit the investigation. Let's pool what we have learned so far and set up a plan of action!"

I smiled and actually felt better, and, inexplicably, my thoughts became more focused on the real problem at hand. "You know," I said, "I actually noticed something else about these murders The newspapers are sure to connect up three similarities in the cases. Bound to. I was a reporter and I have. You probably know already what I'm talking about."

"So, what is it?"

"There's a pattern to these killings besides the fact that all of them involve people on the Blue Book committee."

What is it?"

I counted the points off on the fingers of my right hand, "One, Buffy, a former championship swimmer, dies in what was staged to appear to be a swimming accident; two, Rhinelander Merritt, an author, is stabbed with a letter opener; and three, Melinda Darlington, whose passion was her rose garden, is poisoned by doctored vitamin C made from her own home grown rose hips."

And even more, one of Merritt's books was entitled *The Hampton Society Letters.*"

"Interesting and probably no happenstance. But what could it mean, except that we're dealing with someone with a macabre sense of humor?"

"I wish I knew. Maybe it will help us prevent a fourth murder though. We could warn the remaining committee members so that they could be on their guard.

"And, Walt, something else. When I interviewed Rick at the lighthouse, he mentioned three murders. How could he have learned of that unless he either committed them or had inside knowledge?"

"Remember Alexander Graham Bell's great invention?" asked Walt with a grin.

"Well, maybe. But he's high on my list," I countered.

I promised to find out who on the committee were entrusted with approving or blackballing applicants, and decided to call it a day. It seemed there were perhaps ten, so there would be seven left to be warned, I thought.

"That won't cause a stampede, I'm sure. Let's go ahead with it. Who should we contact?"

"With Melinda dead, Avery would probably take over."

"She was head of the committee?"

"Right. We should probably just contact the other members ourselves. because they're good and nervous. We'll have to call Avery for the names. I don't think I know all of them."

"Won't Frank be pleased with himself," Walt remarked.

"He'll probably apply for his investigator's license," I agreed, "if his theory is right. I won't say that it is, though, until we have absolute proof."

▼

VII

T he next morning, the headlines went wild: MILLION-AIRES TARGETS OF POSSIBLE MADMAN was one tabloid streamer. SOCIALITES IN WEIRD MURDER PLOT read another. Perhaps the worst screamed: 'BLUE BLOOD RUNS RED!' with insets of the three victims and an overall aerial shot of Dune Road mansions

Reporters flocked to the Hamptons and every room at the old Irving Hotel, beloved by visiting dowagers, was taken. Rumors were spreading about a serial killer stalking the posh lawns and boat docks of innocent residents. For the first time since Friday, I was grateful to O'Neill for getting the publicity which might cause possible future victims to be on their guard.

Rather than trouble Avery Darlington, I called his personal secretary and, explaining who I was, asked for the names of the remaining committee members. Since there was actually no secret about who they were, she agreed to read me the list over the phone. The names included Mary Anderson, Robert Lloyd Gardiner Stewart, Emerson Whitwell Smith, Everett St. Oswell, Ethel G. Cooper, Thomas Phillip White, and his wife Honoria Phipson White. Counting Avery, that made eight potential victims. After sleeping on it, I decided against telling all these people that they could be on the killer's gilt-edged list.

What I needed to do was discover who the Blue Book rejects were, and the most direct route to that destination was Mary Anderson. Of the committee members whose names I knew fairly well, Mary seemed the most promising. She was notoriously outspoken. But her confidences were made in such an affable way that her words could rarely be taken as spiteful or bitter.

Unmarried, Mary Anderson lived in the home of her late father, Christopher Anderson, an inventor who had designed his own Gothic masterpiece to live in, complete with towers, turrets, and romantic balconies swathed in Heavenly Blue morning glories. Brown shingle, rather shabby, the old pile had been the abode of genius. Anderson had been a colleague of Edison and was the owner of a number of patents.

His down to earth heirs were the real thing: gentlefolk, kind, generous, modest and unaffected.

As I rang the bell, I thought of the difference between Alexander Hamilton and Thomas Jefferson. The illegitimate man was a snob while the gentleman born to the purple, a true democrat and lover of his fellow man.

All of Anderson's progeny—three sons and two daughters—were well loved by everyone, rich and poor, old and young. Their wealth came from the patriarch's many patented inventions. Most of Anderson's children had left home by now, but Mary remained, seemingly content to remain single in her private palace. Like so many rich women, she feared any would-be suitor was after her millions, not herself.

True to the Anderson nature, it was Ms. Anderson and not a servant who opened the door to greet me. I believe in the surprise visit, a trick dating from my newspaper days.

"Why, it's Liz Grady, isn't it?" she said.

I had forgotten how lovely her cornflower-blue eyes were. They made her seem all the more open and honest. She had curly brown, shoulder-length hair and wore a simple, pale blue dress.

"Yes, it's me, Ms. Anderson. You can call me Liz, if you like."

Ms. Anderson beamed. It was a lovely, friendly smile. "Call me Mary, then."

"It's been some time since we last met at one of Emily Cosgrove's functions," I said. (I used Buffy's formal first name since I remembered that Mary really disliked the society Wasp habit of using nicknames like Muffy, Buffy, and so on, finding them vacuous and phony.) I was trying to find a graceful way to broach the subject.

"Almost a year, I think. Won't you come in?"

"Thank you."

The inside of the Anderson home, in which I'd never been before, was just as livable and unaffected as its owner. Wainscoting, banisters, ceiling beams, doors, lattices, paneling, and moldings were variously made of oak, maple, and cherry. In the two-story foyer, I was delighted to see a large pump organ, and I asked Mary whether it still worked.

"Oh, yes," she answered, "we still use it for weddings, Christmas celebrations, and birthday parties. The pipes run all through the house, which makes it a horrible nuisance to repair and keep clean, so I don't play it too often."

"I'd love to hear you play sometime, but right now I have a more serious matter to discuss."

"Ah, you mean the register murders," she acknowledged, leading the way to a parlor with a sunny view over the ocean.

"That's what the newspaper's calling these killings, yes," I said. The room was decked with oriental carpets and heavy curtains. There was a grand piano in one corner. Over it hung a Mary Cassatt of a mother and child that looked genuine, at least to my untrained eye. Mary sat down on a Louis XIV chair, offering me a place on the comfortable-looking divan. I was then offered iced petits fours and tea. There was a chill ocean breeze, and the Earl Grey tea was comforting.

"I know this is probably intruding on the rules you and the other members have established about protocol," I said after several sips, "but I need to know who might have been up for consideration who was at some point rejected, and whether there was any way this person might have discovered they were being blackballed."

"That would mean a leak among one of the members," Mary said. "It's possible, of course,

Is there anyone in jeopardy now?

She stayed silent for a while, obviously reviewing those she knew. "If you mean being taken off the register because of misconduct, there's one possibility I heard of from Thomas.

"Who's Thomas?"

"Thomas Phillip White, He's a broker, well respected here. Apparently, Mr. Chapelle has been going around trying to induce people to invest in some Los Angeles-based conglomerate. He approached Thomas with his proposal, but his mistake was that Thomas knows quite a lot about that market and knew this was a pretty shaky deal, so he turned down the offer. This caused Mr. Chapelle no end of embarrassment, as he was putting on all these airs about being an expert in the field and so on. But Thomas could probably tell you more about all this than I could, if you're really interested. He and Honoria live in Bridgehampton."

"Maybe I should. Can you remember anything else?"

"Not about Mr. Chapelle, no."

"How about anything about people who've been blackballed.

"Liz, I know I have a reputation for being a bit of a gossip, but I also have a few rules that I don't break. I promised the committee that I would not discuss the issues of the selection process with anyone who was not a member. I'm sorry, but I really feel duty-bound not to reveal any names. However, I don't mind telling you that of the people I can think of who would qualify as being blackballed, none of them seem capable of these murders. In fact, many of them aren't even in this state at the moment."

"I see. Well, I do understand your position."

"I'm sorry, but that's the best I can do. Is there anything else I can do to help?"

"Yes, do you know of anyone else Rafael Chapelle talked to about this investment?"

"I'd be happy to ask around for you and let you know."

"That would be helpful. Thank you, Mary."

I finished my tea, said goodbye, and my hostess escorted me to the door. My next move, I resolved, would be to visit Rafael at his new address.

A maintenance man gave me a lift from Mary's residence to Main Street. I headed for the Village lockup, a temporary holding cell for brief stays. Serious cases went to Riverhead, but Rafael was obviously only in for questioning. The police were able to hold him briefly because of an old DWI complaint he had ignored.

Noticing a car parked across the street with a man in it, I squinted to make out who it was and then started as I recognized the face as belonging to the same man who punched out Richard Hughes at The Drivers Seat, namely Dabney. Realizing I was staring at him, Rick's blacksheep brother started his car and pulled away.

Since I represented a law firm, though it was mainly retained to protect the company which insured Buffy's life as well as her property, the Village police let me see Rafael. The law firm was principally concerned, I thought, in keeping the profitable Cosgrove account no matter who killed Buffy. But, they also wanted to show some interest in her violent death and support of the law enforcement efforts.

A bedraggled Rafael said, "I hope you've come to get me out of here." His usually crisp white shirt looked soiled and his trousers needed pressing. He also needed a shave.

When I murmured, "Not yet," he frowned. "I'm sorry I can't offer you more hospitable accommodations."

I said nothing, but sat down next to him on the bed.

"You know what they say," Rafael continued, "about these are the times when you find out who your true friends are? I've discovered that I have none, and it's a distressing revelation indeed. The only person who has helped me at all is my attorney, and he gets paid to do that."

"If it helps any, Rafael, I don't believe you're guilty."

"You don't?" He smiled again. It was the smile of a small, lost child who has unexpectedly found a new friend. He really was, as Mary classified him, "a harmless, rather pathetic fortune hunter." And now, with Buffy dead, even her fortune had eluded him.

"No, I don't. Of course, it's clear that you didn't kill Melinda Darlington...."

"Yes, I'd heard about that. But they're saying that the two cases aren't related and that I still could have done the first two."

"Except that there is a pattern to these killings that I'm pursuing."

"They'll just cry `copy-cat killer,'" Rafael sighed dramatically.

"Look," I said, growing a little irritated by his interruptions, "the point is that I think I can track down who's really doing this, and if I do that, then you're off the hook."

"Well, then, Godspeed, Liz, Godspeed and bless you. You were always a good friend to dear Buffy,"

"We have to help each other in order to figure out what's happening."

"Very well, but what can I do, stuck in here?"

"I need some information, and you're the best one to fill me in. I understand that you've been trying to get some investors involved in some sort of business venture of yours."

"Oh," said Rafael, "that."

"Yes. What's the name of this company in Los Angeles?"

"You don't know?"

"Would I be asking if I did? Don't think you can take advantage of me because of that, though," I warned. "I can find out a lot of other ways, I just thought I could save myself the trouble by going to the source.

"If you insist. It's called Omnitech Research, a perfectly legitimate, hundred-million-dollar-per-year company that specializes in semiconductor research for the aeronautics industry."

"Mary Anderson told me that you offered Thomas White a chance to recommend Omnitech to his own clients, but he turned you down because it was a bad investment."

"That's just one man's opinion."

"Tell me, Rafael, is this deal the same one you were talking to Richard Hughes about during the night of Buffy's death?"

"Yes," Rafael admitted, "but I really don't see what that has to do with the murders. You just said you know I'm innocent!"

"Maybe it has nothing to do with them," i agreed. But it does seem to be of importance to a number of people. Like Richard Hughes. Anne said that the two of you were arguing that night. So, was it about Omnitech?"

Rafael nodded. "He was upset that and his brother had lost some money after investing in the company. Yes, it was my suggestion that they do so, but I hardly twisted their arms. They're grown men perfectly capable of declining my offer, like Mr. White did."

"And you told White that he should recommend it to his customers, despite that?"

"Yes. But you don't understand. They didn't have enough patience. Sure, Omnitech is losing some money right now, but that's only paper losses, not real money. The company's using some of its profits to invest in technology for the future. So, although right now it looks like their stocks are in bad shape, in a few years it'll be skyrocketing, mark my words!"

"What exactly is Omnitech putting all its money into?"

"Liquid nitrogen technology!" said Rafael excitedly. "Oh, don't ask me to explain all the scientific stuff behind it, but they're researching how super-cold temperatures improve the conductivity of certain metals and other materials. This sort of thing takes years, of course, before it's fully developed."

"I see, and how exactly did you become involved in all of this?"

"Ah, you see, the main laboratory is in Arizona, but Omnitech's business headquarters is in Los Angeles, where for some time I've been involved in a number of other ventures. Through a rather long string of events, I just happened to make contact with some of the other investors and decided to get in on the game."

"And what's your stake in the company?"

"Pardon?"

"Money, Rafael. How much of your own money did you put into this?"

"My dear lady! I'm a consultant, not an investor. I earn my fees by counseling others."

That's what I thought, I said to myself. I was beginning to put together what was happening here, and could safely guess that Rafael had not come to visit his wife simply for love and companionship. He was, more than likely, ducking other irate investors on the West Coast.

"Thanks, Rafael. I'll be talking with you again, I'm sure."

"That's it?"

"I have to get clarification of all our theories and you've got to be proven innocent, right?" I said. "It just needs a dash of cleverness, maybe yours. Keep thinking!"

"I understand," Rafael said reluctantly, "and thank you for your faith in me. I really need someone to care if I live or die."

"I'll contact your lawyer when I have something," I said, and motioned for the guard to open the door.

"Goodbye," Rafael called after me.

I stopped for a copy of The Wall Street Journal; I saw that Rafael's stock had dropped by 1 7/8 since last Friday. Calling Merrill Lynch which had a small office on Main Street, I learned that sales of the stock had been fairly high, as well, so it looked like people were bailing out. Of course, if Rafael was right it would actually be a good time to buy the stock in anticipation of better days ahead. Stocks, however, weren't my strong point, and I really couldn't guess what might be a good investment and what might not. I'd lay down money that it wasn't, though. The whole thing nagged at me. Although I didn't see it clearly at the moment, the circumstances involving the murders and the business with Rafael's Omnitech investments suggested some sort of connection.

I called TJ from the police station. The policemen at the Village PD were picked mainly for looks, I often thought. They were a stunning group, reportedly the highest paid force on Long Island, maybe anywhere.

Once home, I collected the canine contingent and went outside for a walk. The weather was overcast and chilly. A slight drizzle made everything look three shades darker than it actually was. Penn Station took the lead as all three of the dogs pulled at their leashes in order to reach the many fascinating smells that surrounded them as quickly as possible. I had to admit to myself that I hadn't trained them as well as I could have.

Penn Station's leash went limp suddenly, and I almost ran into him where he stood frozen, his nose trained on a scent somewhere ahead and to the right. Seth and Saint followed his lead, and I tried to see what they were noticing. Then I saw it: Mrs. Ary Joyant Dault, walking her Siamese cat and heading toward us.

I quickly ran back to the house and got all three dogs safely inside before returning to Ary Dault and her precious sealpoint.

I joined her and we exchanged a hug. My father had been a great friend of her stockbroker husband, frequently driving him down to his brokerage office and reading the Wall Street Journal to "Lub," who was blind. And my mother and I had been frequent visitors to Thimble Farm where they lived with a number of boarders, all Siamese cats.

I joined Ary and her leashed friend in a stroll down North Sea Road --not so busy in those days as it unfortunately is today.

"I'm thinking of leaving Southampton," she said without preliminary.

She wore a long rusty black skirt, a white satin blouse and a light throw of some kind of soft rose-colored wool. I noticed a few buttons on her blouse were off. But the diamonds on her fingers were real and she had a large emerald holding her collar together. Her cat was on a lavender leash studded with sequins. I looked closer. They were imperfect, but no doubt about it, Bartholomew's leash was diamond-studded.

"I had Stanley drop me and Bartholomew off a block from here," she said. "I hoped to find you in."

I knew she had been touring the islands off the East coast by hydroplane, for some time, clutching the latest in a series of pug dogs, all named Jamie, to her bosom since her dear "'Lub' had died some ten years ago. But now she planned to leave for good, she said.

"They were very mean to 'Lub' here and I haven't forgotten or forgiven, she went on.

Mrs. Dault may have been dropped from the gilt-edged pages of the register after she'd married her husband Lubkert Dault, a Jewish broker, but he had made millions in the market for her before he died, leaving her fabulously rich, with much more money than many of those still featured in Society's listings.

"I may leave Southampton forever," she continued, bending down to pick up some plastic which she put into a large bag she was carrying. Like me, Ary was a conservationist, always adopting highways.

Her arm was muscular, I noticed, mentally resolving to work out more since I was getting flabby. She also walked at a fast athletic pace, forcing Bartholomew and me to run every now and then to keep up with her.

As we watched her cat investigate a spider, she proceeded to pick up a few candy wrappings and a discarded empty beer can.

"What pigs!" she said..

"Thinking of moving to a warmer climate?" I asked.

"It's not the weather, it's the atmosphere. "These people are a lot of bigots really, anti-Semitic and not worthy to kiss 'Lub's ' foot. Well, I'll get back at them"

We were at Thimble Farm. Her guinea hen watchdogs uttered some shrill screams. Guinea hens, Ary maintained, were the best watchmen you could obtain and cheaper to feed than dogs.

As Stanley, a Polish driver, who often picked her up at East Hampton Airport when she returned from one of her island adventures, put it, "She's got it! But, she's close."

"When I was younger, people demonstrated more loyalty to one another. They didn't start accusing people at the drop of a hat," she rambled on, glaring at the guinea hens which were making a racket..."

"Times change," I said uselessly.

"Yes. I'm thinking I might move to Atlantic City, or maybe one of the islands like Nantucket. Probably the former, though. You know how I I like the slot machines and the oceanfront. I can look after 'Lub's' investments better when I'm not mad at everybody."

We walked a little farther in silence.

""Ary,. I said, "do you have theories about these killings yourself. You know the people better than anyone. You made your debut with Millie, didn't you?

"It might help me with the investigation."

"I thought I knew them," she said in a low voice.. "I didn't know how rotten many of them are --not all. Millie and Mary Anderson --people like that are true blue. But now Millie's dead. Maybe Mary will be next?"

"What happens when they take you off the register?"

"What happens? What do you mean?"

"Well, I mean, how do people treat you? Is it very different and uncomfortable?" I laughed, "This is really awkward, I know."

"That's fine," said Mrs. Dault kindly. "I'll see if I can explain it. "You know about how they used to make black people sit in the backs of buses. Socially, it's something like that, just as unfair, ridiculous, Yet, at times it hurts.

"Snobs insist on creating hierarchies, But members of the true upper class are intellectually superior, above this kind of folly. Snob means without nobility. 'sine nobilitae.'"

"Liz, I never felt inferior because I was dumped. I felt superior. And 'Lub' was worth six of them. They'll see!"I wondered if she was the killer.

"What do you mean?" I asked. "They'll see!"

"Why, I just told you. I'm leaving --giving the cats to good homes, taking 'Jamie," and giving New York Hospital a new wing, the Lubkert Dault Pavilion. I'm not giving a dime to Southampton Hospital, the historic society or any of the other groups that are after 'Lub's' money!"She gave me a friendly wave, asked if I wanted Stanley to drive me home, and started down the lane to Thimble Farm where the sink was always full of dirty dishes from fish she cut up for the cats. Raised with servants, Ary Dault had never bothered about mundane matters like housecleaning.

Praying she wasn't a homicidal maniac from all the suffering society and its follies had caused her, I started home.

I sympathized with Mrs. Dault. Her years with her husband had given her a thorough understanding of anti-Semitism—or at least a secondhand one. Whether she was dropped because of her husband's religion, or just because he was an unknown factor with no distinguished lineage to base acceptance on, I certainly didn't know. But I knew she thought his religion was the reason she was eliminated from membership in a kind of exclusive club with emphasis on "exclude."

The pain Ary Dault had gone through was so unnecessary, so absurd, yet very real to her and others like her who had been so randomly ostracized by their peers. I shook my head sadly.

At the house, I dialed the Southampton Hospital, and asked for the coroner.

"Dr. Bellows!" was the answer. This wonderful woman who grew up as a poor fisherman's daughter in Hampton Bays was a favorite family doctor and also subbed as coroner. She once told me that a fellow doctor who belonged to the best clubs told her he couldn't fraternize with her and her peers because she didn't belong. Like Mrs. Dault, she felt scorched by this rejection.

"Hi, Doctor, Liz Grady calling. Anything new on the Millie Darlington autopsy yet?"

"Hello, Liz. Still on the wagon, I hope?"

I told her, "Yes," and laughed. She had helped sober a lot of us up by removing fake diagnoses like 'influenza' from the chart, replacing it with ALCOHOLISM in block letters.

"Congratulations. We just released the results to the deceased's relatives and I can tell you our findings now. Hold on, please."

There was a pause, and I heard the sound of some papers being shuffled. "Here we are. The victim died from an over-dose of anesthetic cocaine."

"Cocaine? I don't understand. There was no evidence that she was an addict."

"Well, there were no traces of cocaine in her nasal passages or lungs. Apparently, she ingested a mega-dose of the stuff. On top of that, she was hypoglycemic. According to her medical records, she's suffered from low blood sugar since she was a teen-ager. Of course, the combination of her pre-existing condition and ingesting drugs was more than enough to send her into cardiac arrest. Her body just couldn't take it."

"I see. Thanks, Dr. Bellows."

VIII

My clients, Higgins, Forsythe and Foster, were beginning to get properly anxious for a report. I could tell this by the way Tom Daly called me a few minutes after I'd gotten off the phone with the coroner's office and told me they expected a written report on my progress by the day after tomorrow. This was the one thing I hated about working for big clients. Although they could afford your services, they insisted on slowing you up by adding paperwork to the list of tasks you had to do; then they complained that you were taking too long to complete the investigation. I typed up a brief, two-page summary and took it to the Federal Express office, making certain to keep the receipt to add to my expense report. Then I came back home and called Walt.

"Walt, it's me, Liz."

"Hi, Liz! How are you doing? Are you calling about dinner arrangements, I hope?"

"No. You know, for someone who's always thinking about fitness, you sure are preoccupied with food."

"Deprivation does that to you."

"That's what I thought. Anyway, I need your help again."

"Sure, Liz. What's up?"

"I need someone to go to the station and check the narcotics squad records on the people who were at the Darlington's party. See if any of them have a record of drug use—specifically, cocaine." Briefly, I explained to Walt what had killed Mrs. Darlington. "I can't do it myself, and I know Detective O'Neill won't help me out. I was hoping maybe

Chief Walker owes you a favor and you could convince him to get you access to the files."

"That's a pretty tall order. It would mean having to work around O'Neill."

"Yeah, I know. So, you don't think you can do it?"

"I didn't say that."

"And check under the names of all the staff at the Darlington house, too, while you're at it—and check Mr. Darlington. We might as well cover all the bases."

"That'll take a while." Walt paused to consider his strategy. "Okay, give me a couple hours. I'll call you back."

"Thanks, Walt."

Walt switched back to his favorite subject. "Is dinner still on?",

"Let's try the Lobster Inn!" Ever since I covered the rescue of the owner and a worker after their boat overturned in the rough waters of Shinnecock Bay and they got swept out into the Atlantic, spending the night hanging onto their overturned boat, I liked to visit this restaurant on Peconic Bay. After covering the dramatic rescue by a Grumman plane piloted by the assistant's father, I knew that the owner had to have a business administration degree. When I met him in person for an interview on his miraculous escape, sure enough, he did have one from Bucknell.

How did I know? He built the restaurant from driftwood and did his own fishing! How's that for an economical operation?

The phone rang. Walt was reporting on his research. "I talked to Walker and he agreed to get O'Neill to stay out of the way and give me access to the files."

"Great. Thanks a lot, Walt. I realize that couldn't have been very easy. Had to do a lot of maneuvering?"

The only catch is you can't come along. I'll have to go through the records myself."

I shrugged this off. "Doesn't matter to me how it's done,

just as long as it is. Be sure to check the names of the Darlingtons' staff, too"

It was less than an hour later that the phone rang again. Walt reported that no one in the case had a record for the sale or use of drugs. No addicts or pushers among the persons involved.

"Okay, Walt. Thanks. I really appreciate how helpful you've been."

"Wish I could've given you something useful like a lead. I can't believe how frustrating this case is."

"Tell me about it. I'll talk to you later, okay?"

"Later? When?"

"I don't know when." I was beginning to get irritated at Walt's constant insisting. "We've both got a lot of work to do, and I realize I've been keeping you from yours How about this weekend, I'll see you then."

Walt mumbled assent, and hung up the phone. He sounded a little hurt, but I needed some time. Evidence was scanty and it seemed to me there was only one possible source of pay dirt on who would have a motive: Mary Anderson. Wondering whether I'd get the brush-off, I dialed her number.

"Mary? This is Liz. Sorry to disturb you again, but I could use your help still."

"Oh, yes, Liz. I've been making some queries for you about those people we were discussing, but I'm afraid I haven't had much luck in turning up anything."

"That's all right. Thank you for trying. May I ask you something? I understand that the committee keeps detailed histories of all the people who are listed in the Blue Book or have been considered for inclusion. Is that correct?"

"Yes, it is."

"Do you know where those records are kept?"

"Well, some of them are in the archives at the Rogers Memorial Library. Mrs. Darlington, poor dear, was chairper son, but she can't help you. A lot of them were with Mr. Merritt when he died."

"What do you mean `were'?"

"Well, I mean that many of the ones he was researching are missing now. Didn't you know?"

"No, I didn't!" My thoughts were spinning. "Do you know which ones are missing?"

"Yes. They were some records dating back many years. Unfortunately, we hadn't enough foresight to make copies of them, and now they're lost forever. The only thing that's left from that period are committee minutes, which are still kept at the library. It's really a shame."

"Yes. Do you have any idea why someone would want those records?"

"No, not really. It's not like they were of any material value—just historical."

"I see. How strange."

"Do you have any ideas what this might all mean?" Mary asked. "Is it connected to these murders?"

"I think it is somehow,

Mary sounded troubled, "Do you think you're getting any closer?"

"I'm still working on it. Mary, do you know whether anyone can gain access to those archive files?"

"You certainly can, but you have to get approval from a committee member first."

"Like you, Mary?"

"If you like. Yes, I can get you in. I just have to talk to the librarian."

We agreed to meet at the library at two o'clock, which left me enough time for a quick cheese sandwich and soda. I met Mary by the periodical displays. I suddenly realized that, like all of us, Mary was getting old. I saw some crow's feet lines around her eyes and wrinkles across her usually serene forehead.

She was wearing a severe black suit with a ruffled white blouse. Actually, Mary looked like a librarian herself. But a librarian's salary would never have covered the necklace she wore of matched emeralds.

The librarian led us downstairs. The archive room was actually a glorified walk-in closet with a reinforced, fireproof door way back in the corner of the magazine storage area, where only the periodicals librarian dared to tread. It was dimly lit here, and the archive room was even worse, only one light bulb provided illumination.

The archive room was stuffed with old journals and logs dating back to the mid-nineteenth century. Dusty tomes with brittle leather covers and stiff, yellowing pages lined the walls and aisles and were stacked up to precarious heights on the floor and on top of the room's only table.

I looked around miserably. "I don't even know where to begin," I protested.."

"That's not a problem. I used to work in this library," Mary said, (I was right, I thought. She actually was a librarian.)

Pointing to a shelf where a set of books numbered with Roman numerals was squeezed between two metal bookends, she explained, "These are the minutes to the committee meetings. They cover the same period as the stolen records.

We each took a stack of the oversized books off the shelf, set them down on the table, and began the laborious process of paging through the minutes in the hopes of finding a correlation between the victims and the missing records from Merritt's yacht. For over an hour we scanned the deteriorating pages without success until I reached a familiar name,: Miss Ary Joyant Stevenson.

"Mary," I almost shouted, "come look at this!" I pointed out the citation in the entry. "Did you know that Mrs. Dault had been a member of the Blue Book committee?"

"No, I didn't," she said. "I've never heard anyone mention it before. I wonder why it was such a secret."

"I don't think it was a secret. She probably just preferred to avoid the subject after she was blackballed."

"Oh, yes. That does make some sense. And look, here's Mrs. Darlington." Mary pointed to a name on the page.

"It says Melinda Blackburn. Her maiden name?"

"Yes. She's been on the committee forever. I mean, was," Mary corrected.

"I wonder if any other familiar names appear in the membership listings. Mary, I think we can get through this quickly by just scanning the beginning of each entry for the list of attendees."

"Right. I'll get to it."

Mary returned to her stack and I went back to mine. It was only another ten minutes or so before a third name appeared: Lawrence Cosgrove, Buffy's father. Only a few months further into the entry, the last name clicked into place: Tristan Merritt.

"Was Tristan Merritt Rhinelander's father?" I asked Mary.

"No," said Mary. "I think he was an uncle or something like that."

"Mary," I grinned, "I think we have our connection. The murderer isn't working in the present, he's revenging himself on the past!" I looked down at the entry, dated back a generation or so.

"Now the question is, what occurred back all those years ago which would be enough to cause a descendant to commit murder? And why did the killer just act now?"

"Well, I don't have any idea," said Mary. I reviewed the names on the page again. One of them was Christopher Anderson. I didn't say anything about it to Mary, however.

"Mary, would it be okay if I photocopied this page?"

Mary nodded, "If you're careful."

I assured her I would be, and took the book upstairs to the photocopier, where I inserted two dimes for two copies. I returned to the archive room and put the volume back on the shelf with the rest of the books that Mary had already replaced.

"Thank you again for all your help, Mary," I said. "This has really gone a long way toward a possible conviction."

"Well, I'm glad to help. Perhaps you could do me a small service in return?"

"Sure."

"Could you see what you can do about getting me some police protection?" Mary covered her mouth with one hand for a moment before continuing: "You see, I noticed my father's name on the minutes. You think I'm going to be one of the victims, don't you?"

"It's still just a working theory, Mary. There might not be anything to it."

"You seemed pretty certain about it a minute ago."

"Yes, I did, didn't I." I sighed, "To be honest, Mary, I don't think I could convince the Southampton police to come out to your house. But I know what I can do."

"What?"

"I'll come out and stay with you a while, and I'll bring a friend of mine who's a detective in Sag Harbor, where they're also investigating the killings."

Mary looked visibly relieved. "That would be fine with me, Liz. Thank you. There's plenty of room in my home. I'm the only one there, as you know. I'll make sure you're comfortable, and you won't have to stay too long. I'll call my brothers, and I'm certain one of them will be able to come out in a few days from Seattle and keep me company until this all blows over."

"Of course. It's no bother for me at all." I'd have to board the animals at the Old Towne Animal Hospital on Hampton Road, but that small inconvenience was hardly justification for refusing Mary's request.

She readily agreed to drive me back to my house so that I could make a few arrangements, and about an hour later we were back at her home, where she had her cook fix us a vegetarian banquet of creole rice with fresh mushrooms.

"We had already finished eating when Walt knocked at the door and Mary let him in.

"Sorry it took me so long to get here," he said.

The alarm system was activated. Mary gave us the secret code since should we want to go out or return in, we would need the code.

I had a 32 caliber hand gun and I knew Walt had his standard issue revolver.

It was still early, but Mary wasn't a night owl and liked to retire by 9. We reassured her that we would take turns on watch during the night.With the lights in the house dimmed or turned off, everyone retired except for Walt and me,

"Do you really think the murderer's going to try to kill her next?" he asked in a low voice.

I pulled out one of the photocopies of the old committee minutes I'd made earlier. "This is the list of names I told you about over the phone." I pointed the names out one by one: "Here's Buffy's father, Merritt's uncle, and Mrs. Darlington. They appear on this list exactly in the same order in which they were killed. And the next name on the list is Christopher Anderson, Mary's father."

"Almost like the killer's working from a shopping list," Walt commented.

"Exactly. Merritt must have had a photocopied page or other duplicate with him in his boat cabin. So let's work from this scenario: The murderer has some kind of vendetta against the members of that period, people who were on the committee at the time.

1. "That information is available only to committee members. Learning that Rhinelander Merritt has a copy because he's doing research for his next novel, the murderer visited Merritt's yacht. Once on the vessel, he gained access to the papers, perhaps by force, and, either already aware that there was a Merritt on the list or discovering this fact upon seeing the names, decided to kill Merritt—but not immediately. He forced Merritt to telephone Buffy at home, asking her to meet

him on the yacht. "Lonely and bored, Buffy complied, quite possibly because she was fascinated by Merritt's brilliance. She may have expected a midnight swim since Merritt himself was an excellent swimmer and diver

"After a few drinks, Buffy loved to swim at night. Dangerous, but she claimed it was the best hangover remedy known. So, she wore a bathing suit under a loose wrap. The wrap has never turned up and is probably at the bottom of the ocean by now.

I paused for breath and from a silver tray the thoughtful Mary had left us, poured Walt and myself some hot coffee, while marshaling my ideas.

The surf outside the windows roared. I looked out and saw a full moon silvering the waves. A path of diamonds extended to the horizon. In the far distance a fog horn sounded. moaning like the voices of ghosts. Beautiful, mysterious.

Clearing my throat I looked over at Walt and tried to pick up the threads of the way it worked, as I visualized it. "By the time she arrived, Merritt was probably already dead. Or maybe he killed her first. But he didn't want the two murders to be associated with each other—at least, not right away."I think he put Buffy's body in the boat and took her in her own motor boat from Sag Harbor into Great Peconic Bay through the Shinnecock Canal into Shinnecock Bay. Then they entered the Atlantic Ocean through the inlet.

He dumped her out in front of her own home and then sent the speed boat out to sea. He or she has to be a top swimmer, familiar with these waters, probably a native."He nodded agreement.

"That sounds like the right scenario. By native, you don't mean a Shinnecocker, do you?"

"No, not an Indian. Someone who has summered out here for years or lives here all year round. Someone familiar with the tides."

Walt, stretching on a green satin sofa, looked at me, laughed and said, "Well, if you won't marry me, at least, listen to my ideas now about the third murder, poor old Millie Darlington. I had a professor by that name at Hofstra, Dr. Oscar Gilpin Darlington, by the way."

"It has to be someone who had access to anesthetic cocaine. Possibly someone who works at or has privileges at a hospital or drug store.

"Maybe, he went on, "someone involved with pharmaceuticals. Wasn't that stock Rafael was peddling involved somehow with drugs?"

I thought I heard something, and interrupted him.

"Walt, I thought I heard glass breaking.. Let's look around!"

"It might be a good idea to show ourselves anyway, as long as we stick together."

As we tiptoed along an upstairs hall, Walt stopped and embraced me.

A yellow light flashed in our direction. We looked up to see Mary's butler staring at us disapprovingly from his private room.

"It's a new investigative technique," Walt assured the man. The butler glared at us for a second, said nothing, and closed his door.

"Walt!" I chided.

"Liz!" Walt mocked.

I stifled a laugh, "Okay, come on. This is no time to play around."

"Agreed," said Walt. "Let's check out the third floor"

We finished our tour without incident and went back down to the parlor for some more caffeine. There was a fresh pot of coffee on the sideboard for us.

I picked up a cup of coffee and strolled over to a long French window, overlooking the garden.

Then every muscle in my body tensed up. I nudged Walt, who almost spilled his coffee. "Did you see that?"

"See what?"

I waited a second, then it was there again, a dark shadow crossing over to the left. "There!"

"Yes, I see it!"

We wasted no time. Running back into the kitchen, Walt threw open the door, setting off the security siren, which blared louder than a car alarm. House lights suddenly blazed, as Walt and I ran toward the yard where we had seen the intruder. Again, I saw the dark figure, running across a long stretch of lawn, on the other side of which was a cluster of trees.

I yelled, "Stop or I'll shoot!" And I fired a warning shot into the air.

Walt shouted, "Police!"

But the intruder ignored us and kept running. He was heading for the trees and reached them about five seconds before we did. Walt motioned me to go to the right of the trees instead of through them. "Watch it, Liz. Go around."

I veered to the right as Walt went left, fearing that we'd lost our man. The night was very dark with the moon hidden behind some clouds now and only some hazy illumination from the house. Reaching the other side of the trees, I paused to get my bearings when I heard a car engine turn over on my left. Spinning around, I was blinded by a pair of bright headlights that switched on just as I was facing the car.

"Liz! Watch out!"

The engine roared. Tires churned in the grass.

The headlights jumped toward me and I threw myself as hard as I could into the bushes.

"Liz!"

The sound of our suspect making his escape in his car faded away faster than the sound of my heart beating wildly.

Walt was next to me in an instant. I was lying in a pile of thistles and twigs, scratched and scared, but otherwise unhurt.

"Are you hurt?" Walt asked, not daring to help me up quite yet. "Should I call an ambulance?"

"No, I'm not hurt, just a few bruises and cuts."

I stood up, though a little wobbly at the knees. Taking a few deep breaths to steady my nerves, I reassured Walt I was fine, but couldn't conceal my frustration. "We almost had him, Walt! And we were right, he was after Mary."

"You mean you were right," said Walt.

"Whatever. Did you see a license plate?"

"No. He had it covered up with mud or duct tape or something. I did see that he was driving an old two tone station wagon, maybe a Plymouth..

"That's okay. It's a start. We're on to him, Walt. That's good, except now he knows we are, so he's not likely to make the same mistake again."

▼

X

After returning to the house, and reassuring Mary that everything was under control and she was in no danger, Walt called the police and reported the incident. It wasn't difficult for him at that point to convince O'Neill over the phone that Mary deserved some protection, so about an hour later a car pulled up to the house with two plainclothes officers who took over for Walt and me. Since it was not too likely that the intruder would return that night, we left.

As usual when a call came from Dune Road, the officers were young and handsome enough to be in the movies.

Back home, we went out in the darkness and in silence, listened to the waves ripple along the surface of the pond and the rustle of the wind in the old swamp maple.

A little later, refreshed in spirit, we wandered into the house together in a mood of total harmony.

In the soft glow of the moon which had come out from its canopy of clouds, we left ourselves completely open and vulnerable to each other that night, and although I had loved Walt deeply and passionately before then, I had never given myself so fully to him.

We held each other in the darkness, not needing to say anything. It was enough that we at last were united in body and spirit.

I slept a dreamless sleep.

A morning thunderstorm brought me back to reality with an electric flash and the cracking blow of sky slamming shut behind a lighting bolt.

I sat up in my bed before I was even awake. My heart pounded in my chest for several beats before it calmed down. Walt, who was a sound sleeper, was breathing softly next to me and his presence put me at ease. I decided to get up and fix him breakfast for a change. It was seven o'clock and time to get moving. Putting on my slippers, I grabbed the morning paper and went into the kitchen with good intentions when a headline at the bottom of the front page caught my eye: "Rites Held For Slain Socialite."

Buffy's funeral had been held yesterday. Strong twinges of guilt plucked at my conscience. Nobody had bothered to call me about the funeral, but I could have easily checked the time and gone to say my last goodbyes.

I resolved to go to the cemetery that day.

A movement at the edge of my vision distracted me from the paper, and I turned to see Walt standing in the entryway to the hall. He had gotten fully dressed while I read the story about the funeral. A mass had been celebrated at Sacred Hearts of Jesus and Mary, the large Catholic church on Hill Street. Buffy was a convert. The funeral was handled by the Brockett Service with burial in Sacred Hearts Cemetery.

Good morning, Sweetheart!" Walt greeted me.

"Hi, Hon," I replied, blowing him a kiss.

We really should go to the cemetery this morning, Walt. Pay our last respects to Buffy!"

"Isn't the funeral today?"

"Yesterday. I completely forgot to check.

Walt walked up behind me and squeezed my shoulders reassuringly. "You've been close to her all along, working to solve her murder. That's a lot better than sending some flowers and crying a lot. So don't feel guilty. Just go and do what you need to do."

"Thanks. Could you run an errand for me while I go?"

"Sure thing."

"Check the DMV records and see if you can narrow down the ancient Plymouth station wagons owners in this area. The driver may have a lot of violations. It's a long shot, I know."

"Will do. That was already on my list anyway."

The weather was perfect for such a sad mission. Rain was falling in a steady gray curtain. I got T.J. to stop his cab at Flowers & Company and picked up a pretty nosegay of white roses, something she would have loved.

Buffy's fresh grave was near that of Gary Cooper. The actor's remains were moved from a Los Angeles graveyard to Sacred Heart Cemetery at the wish of his widow, Veronica Converse, who though remarried, never forgot Gary. She moved him so that she and his daughter, Maria, could visit his grave. A large rose-colored boulder of natural rock marked his resting place.

An enormous, soggy wreath wept over the fresh earth. With some chagrin, I realized that the modest bouquet I had brought would soon be ruined by the rain as well.

As I approached, I could see Cindy from Rick Hughes' office. Strangely, she was slowly circling the grave, staring at the ground as if she were searching for a contact lens. When I was close enough to call to her without shouting in an irreverent way, I said, "Cindy? It's Liz."

Cindy smiled wanly, "Oh, Liz. I didn't notice you coming." The sound of the rain beating on our umbrellas made her voice sound oddly muffled.

"I didn't expect to see anyone here. I wasn't able to attend the services yesterday, so I thought I'd come now. I didn't know you knew Buffy."

"I just knew her as one of our clients, actually. Rick and I came by yesterday."

"So, may I ask why are you here now?"

"Well, it's the craziest thing. I seem to have lost the wallet from my purse. I misplaced it yesterday and ever since I've been going back over all of my steps to see whether I might have dropped it somewhere. Coming here was sort of a last resort."

"I'll help you look," I offered.

"You don't need to bother. I've been all over this place and there's no sign of it. I'm really at my wits end."

"Maybe you didn't drop it, then. Maybe somebody stole it."

"There hasn't been any opportunity for that," said Cindy. "Except for being here, I've either been at home with my husband or at the office. When I'm at work, I keep my purse locked in my desk drawer. I must have just dropped it or left it somewhere. But my money and credit cards are lost. I better get going back to the office so I can report my cards stolen. I'm just on my lunch break. Goodbye, Liz."

My intuition was kicking in again. "Wait, Cindy. Can you give me five minutes and I'll join you."

"You want to come to the office with me?"

"Sure. Maybe I can help."

"I appreciate that, Liz, but you really don't have to bother."

"No, really. I want to."

"Well," Cindy hesitated. "Okay. You can't stay too long, though. My bosses will get upset."

"I won't get in the way," I promised.

"I'll just wait in my car, then."

Cindy walked back to the access road and I turned my attention back to Buffy's final resting place. I said a Hail Mary for the onetime glamour girl and thought of that poem by Shakespeare, "Golden lads and girls all must, as chimney-sweepers, come to dust."

I called to T.J. that I had a ride and he nodded and took off. I'd pay him next time around and that would be soon since I don't drive. Every time I took out a permit as a working alcoholic--I'd see a dead child in the rain. A big deterrent to moving on from Learner's Permit to License.

"Things are awfully tense at Hughes lately, "Cindy informed me.

"Things haven't been going well, I know."

"That's an understatement." Cindy stopped me before we left the car.

"Don't tell anyone I told you this, but the Hughes brothers are through. Rick bought out Dabney and threw him out."

"You're kidding me! Why would Dabney stand still for that?"

"He had to. Rick said it was either that or he would sell his controlling interest to another company that would have thrown Dabney out anyway. At least this way, Dabney can tell people he chose to sell out to his brother and leave with some dignity "

"Wow. I didn't think Rick had the money to do something like that, the way he was talking to me the other day."

"It took every cent he had and a second mortgage on his house," said Cindy, "and if he doesn't turn things around quick, he's going to lose the firm anyway. There're some vultures eyeing us for a hostile take over." Cindy double checked to see that nobody had been listening to our conversation and then led the way to the office building.

Once inside, we checked around the cubicles, in the lunchroom, and in the bathroom for Cindy's wallet without avail.

"I've really got to get back to my desk," said Cindy at last. "I promised Barb that she wouldn't have to hold down the fort for more than an hour."

"Okay. One quick question before you go, though. Does anyone else have a key to the drawer where you keep your purse?"

"Only Rick and Dabney. Each has a master key that unlocks everything in the office."

"Well, I hate to propose this, but as Sherlock Holmes said, when you've eliminated all other possibilities, the last possi bility remaining, no matter how unlikely, must be the solution."

"You think one of the Hughes brothers did it?" Cindy asked incredulously.

"It looks that way," I said. "But let's not make any accusations until we've thought this through a bit more."

"Don't worry about that! They'd fire me in a minute if I said anything like that." We walked over to the reception desk, and Cindy relieved Barb, a pneumatic blonde wearing a red jumper with a gold locket drawing attention to her most visible assets.

I was just about to say good-bye, when Dabney walked in, and I finally got a good look at the man who'd been spying on me at the gas station. Thinner and taller than his brother, Dabney had a high forehead that continued to his neck. What remained of his hair was still a sandy brown, however, and his face was younger than his brother's. The advantage he had in years wasn't enough to make him better looking.

Whereas one could honestly say that Rick was handsome with his square jaw and Roman nose, his brother had a weak chin, unusually narrow nose, and small, shifty eyes. One would almost doubt that they were related so closely, except that their mouths were similar, and when Dabney spoke he sounded remarkably like Rick.

"I've just come back to pick up a few things, Cindy," Dabney announced as he stood next to me without giving me a single glance. He was carrying two empty cardboard boxes.

"Mr. Hughes!" said Cindy. "I wasn't expecting you in today."

"I left in such a rush, I wasn't able to collect all my personal things. Could you let me into my office? I don't seem to have my key," he added ironically.

"Of course. Let me find it for you." Cindy dug inside a drawer and pulled out a silver key with a red plastic tag on it.

"Mr. Hughes," I broke in, seeing an opportunity, "my name's Liz Grady. I was wondering if I could have a moment of your time."

104

"Time is all I have at the moment, Mrs. Grady.". "Aren't you the detective investigating Buffy Cosgrove's death?"

"Yes. That's what I wanted to talk to you about."

"Why me? I don't know anything about it. Didn't you talk to my brother? He's the one who handled Mrs. Cosgrove's portfolio."

"I did talk to him, but this is a very complex case, and I'd like to explore every angle possible."

Dabney regarded me a moment while Cindy waited patiently at his office door, key at the ready. "

"Cindy, if it's OK, I'll chat with Ms. Grady in my old office?"

"Sure, Mr. Hughes."

Cindy let us into the room, which now only contained a desk, two chairs, and some bookshelves with a few scattered books and knickknacks. On the wall, a portrait of a distinguished-looking man whom I guessed to be Dabney's stepfather stared blankly at us.

"What did you wish to talk to me about, Mrs. Grady?" said Dabney as he put the boxes on his desk and began to clean off the shelves.

Actually, I didn't have a clue. I didn't think he'd play along with me anyway, so I decided to play it safe.

"There's no need for you to be concerned, Mr. Hughes. I'm just asking everyone I can about these homicides to see if it will lead to any insights."

"Sounds reasonable," said Dabney without making any eye contact.

"Yes, well, anyway, I know that your company handled affairs for Buffy, maybe Rhinelander Merritt and Millie Darlington. Do you recall any fears anyone expressed? Any concern about possible revenge for barring somebody with social ambitions?"

"Hughes & Associates has hundreds of clients," Dabney said. "I knew very few of them personally. No one said anything but 'How's my stock doing?'" I knew the Darlingtons, as well as Buffy Cosgrove, but only barely. I didn't know Rhinelander Merritt."

Dabney looked at his watch; on his forehead I could see beads of perspiration.

"Now, if you'll excuse me, I've got to run!" Dabney stacked one box on top of the other and headed out the door.

I chased after him, calling, "Mr. Hughes, I'd like to speak with you again later, when you have the time." He continued on past Cindy's desk without so much as a "Goodbye" and bumped into a chair as he left the office.

After Dabney had left, I saw something next to the chair he had stumbled into. Bending down to pick it up, I saw immediately what it was and could barely keep myself from choking.

"Cindy, could I ask you an off-the-wall question?" I asked, straightening up again and carefully wrapping my prize in a handkerchief, which I placed in my purse.

"Sure, Liz."

"What kind of car does Dabney drive?"

"Um, it's a silver Caddy, I think. Yes, that's right, I'm certain it is."

"Does he have more than one car?"

"He did, but I remember him saying he sold it a few months ago."

"Thanks, Cindy. I'll stop bothering you now. Hope you find your wallet!"

I rushed out of the door, leaving Cindy with a puzzled look on her face.

T.J. drove me home, as usual. I paid him for this and the other trip, and after walking the dogs, went off for a walk around the lake.

The fog crept in. The world sank away. Suddenly, the sound of someone running startled me and I turned around to see a figure in dark clothes, ski mask, and gloves charging me.

There was no one else in sight. The lakeside was totally deserted.

In an instant he was on me and instinct took over. He tried to grab my throat.

Screaming as loudly as I could for help, I pulled out a short blackjack I had in a deep pocket in my light cotton jacket, and with all my strength whacked him on the head with it. He fell and I sprinted off in the other direction..

This attack I reported promptly to the police. A friend from newspaper days, Chief Hanscom showed up with Walt --these fellows have a wire into each other, so I wasn't surprised."

To the first question, could I describe my assailant, I had to admit, "No. He or she --it could have been a woman --was wearing a ski mask."

"Damn! Do you think it was the same one who nearly ran you down last night?"I thought so, but had no proof at all.

"Was that driver wearing a mask, too?"

"He might've been. I only saw the back of his head, and it was awfully dark. There was a moon, but the clouds covered it. Visibility was zero."

I told them about my visit to Hughes office. Then, I pulled out the item I'd picked up in Dabney's former office. handed it to O'Neill, and Walt came closer to inspect it as well.

"It's coke," said O'Neill.

"That's right," I said. "Dabney Hughes dropped it as he was leaving his office. He's been freebasing cocaine."

"You think Dabney Hughes is the murderer?" Walt asked.

"Wait a minute," said Chief Hanscom who headed the Southampton Town police. They took in North Sea where I lived. "Let's not jump to any conclusions. Even if we can prove possession, that's not going to help this case any. There is no case for possession anyway. There's a break in the chain of evidence. How could we prove that the coke belonged to him? Anyone could have dropped it. They could say it was planted."

"I know, I know," I said. "I need something better. But I do remember Avery Darlington mentioning that Dabney Hughes was his stock broker and that he had visited the Darlingtons the night before Millie's death. Everyone else who was there, as far as we know, is clean. I still don't have a motive if it was Dabney. But let me see if I guess this right. Walt, how'd it go at the DMV."

"I almost forgot to tell you. There was only one car registered in the Southampton area that met the description we were looking for, and—"

"Let me guess," I interrupted. "It was reported stolen yesterday."

Walt paused. "That's right."

"Certainly fits my theory so far."

"Okay," said Hanscom. "I'll start checking into this guy. In the meantime, you should back off. He left and we settled back to a discussion of my attacker."

The cow bell rang. Walt answered the door and came back with Rafael in tow. He looked disheveled, but sympathetic.

"I got sprung. They admitted I'm not a suspect. Judge Mercator Kendrick let me go on the old DWI charge with a warning. Like you, I'll be using cabs for a while. No driving. I heard about your narrow escape on WLNG so I had to come by to thank you in person, and give you these." He handed me a bouquet of wonderfully fragrant peonies, among my favorites.

"Rafael," I said. "I think you may really get your act together. Basically, you're not a bad guy."

Laughing, he added, "Yes. And now I'll really have to go to work. I may wind up driving a cab myself--in Southampton summers and Palm Beach winters. I'll meet a lot of my old friends."

"Meanwhile," he hesitated. Is there anyway I may show my appreciation? I mean it. Anything I could do?" You believed in me when no one else did."

I thought. "Actually, there is."

"Really? What?"

Finally, something constructive to do. "You could tell me more about Dabney Hughes. When did you first meet him?"

Rafael sat down in the kitchen with Walt at his side and me facing him.

"Oh, you know, at one of those parties Buffy was always holding. This one was the weekend before she died. He was there with his brother."

"Is that when you interested him in Omnitech?"

"Oh, no. I had talked to him on the phone before then. No, he had already bought his stock about two months before then."

"I see. That makes sense. Tell me, Rafael, how well do you know Dabney."

"What do you mean?"

"I'm looking for some character insight here. I only met him once, and Rick probably won't give me a very objective description."

Rafael thought for a second. "I'd say he's kind of a preoccupied fellow. Not too dynamic, either, if you know what I'm saying. But you get the idea that something's always going on in his head that's more important to him than interacting with anybody outside his private little world. His brother is much more interesting and nice to be around."

"Would you think that Dabney was a drug addict."

"Drugs? Like what kind of drugs?"

"Coke."

" I never really thought of that, but that would explain why his nose is always running and why he's supposed to be a rich stock broker, but he drives a run-down Cadillac. He probably snorts most of his salary."

"Okay. He's low on money and tries to make it back by investing his firm's money in stocks in the hopes—we'll speculate—of reaping some of the profits himself? That doesn't sound like quite the picture Rick was painting of his brother. Rick was telling me that it was more like crazed ambition with Dabney, like he was trying to prove he was better than Rick or maybe his stepfather."

"His stepfather," said Rafael as if he just remembered something. "That's another thing about Dabney I noticed. He talked about his stepfather a lot. Got pretty boring."

"He has a portrait of his stepfather in his office," I said. "Sounds kind of obsessive to me."

"Yeah." Rafael suddenly looked guilty.

"What is it?"

"Well, when Dabney found out how much the Omnitech stocks were dropping, he came over to the house and started yelling at me. Then he started crying and wailed about his stepfather never forgiving him. Something crazy like that."

"And it was after that that Rick came over for dinner?" I asked.

Rafael nodded, "That night. I tried to be civilized about it. After all, there was nothing I could do to help. Dabney had invested the money and lost it fair and square. But Rick's like any big brother, I guess, and wouldn't accept that Dabney was at fault. He started screaming lawsuit and criminal investigation and that sort of thing. Buffy and I tried to calm him down, but it just got worse. No wonder she took the first opportunity she had to hightail it out of there."

"By the way, Rafael," I said. "You seem a lot nicer and down to earth!"

"Guess prison changed me back to my old ways, Liz."

"Come on, you weren't there that long."

"Well, then, I guess maybe it's because I feel comfortable around you. I don't talk like a rich snob when I'm in L.A. Just around here where I'm surrounded by them. I don't belong here, I know, but it was fun to try. Now that Buffy's gone and she didn't leave me anything, I'll be going back West. Goodbye, Liz."

"Goodbye, Rafael. Try not to get into anymore trouble."

Rafael grinned, "I'll try, but I won't make any promises."

XII

I called 728-3400, asked to speak to Chief Hanscom. I loved a poster he kept over his desk. Showing a gaggle of geese, the legend underneath read, "LEAD, FOLLOW, OR GET OUT OF THE WAY." I was visualizing that as I asked him if he'd gotten anywhere with Dabney.

"We really don't have much evidence on him."

"What about the clothing fibers? Did I manage to grab any when I was attacked?"

"Yes you did, actually. You must have put up a real fight."

"I was fighting for my life."

Walt looked grim. "I know. I wish I'd been there. This would never have happened to you if I had been."

"Don't blame yourself, Walt. Believe me, I've been down that road. We can't always be joined at the hip, however enjoyable that may be."

"Yeah, whether it's Dabney or not, why you?"

"The only reason I can think of," I speculated, "is that I'm getting too close to the answers. That's another reason I think it could be Dabney. Think about it. Up until now, our murderer's been very clever. Each time he kills, he leaves no evidence behind. Until suddenly something goes wrong that shakes him up: his brother kicks him out of his partnership in the business and he loses his financial security as well as, maybe, a brother. Then he starts to make mistakes. The night following the day he gets fired, he decides to continue with his plan to murder the people on his list. But his confidence is gone, and he almost allows himself to get caught. The next day, what should happen but that one of the people who was chasing him shows up at his former office and tries to question him. He realizes that he's closer to being found out, and his nervousness causes him to leave an important clue. Maybe he even realizes he's dropped it, but he's too scared to go back and pick it up. He's got to try to cut his losses, so he attacks me to try to block the investigation."

"Seems feasible," Walt admitted. "But it's still all speculation." He shrugged, "Maybe Hanscom who's a real brain can find something --some real evidence."

With some befuddled idea of looking over what little evidence Hanscom had, I asked Walt to drive me to the Southampton Town Police on Old Riverhead Road.

I was waiting in the anteroom when Rick showed up.

His handsome features distorted with rage, he bent over me and said, ""Well, if it isn't the person who's accusing my brother of these horrible murders."

"I ... I'm sorry, Rick. I'm just trying to do my job."

"Yes, that's what all the Nazis said after the war, too."

"Come on, Rick. I'm no Nazi."

"What do you call all this intimidation, then?" asked Rick. He refused to sit down next to me when I gestured to him to do so. "You have absolutely no evidence that he's done anything wrong."

"They're just questioning him right now, Rick. Does he have a lawyer, by the way."

Rick nodded, "I contacted one for him, yes. He's in the room with them right now protecting Dabney's rights." He paused. "I never suspected you would do anything like this, Liz. Do you honestly think my brother is a killer?"

"I don't know. I hope not for your sake, as well as his."

"That's what I thought. It's all circumstantial. There's really nothing you have that can point an accusing finger at Dabney, is there?"

"There's his drug habit ...," I began.

"Hey, I'm aware Dabney has some problems and that I had to throw him out because of them, but that doesn't mean anything more than that. It's nothing that some counseling can't straighten out."

"Is he undergoing therapy?" I asked.

"He just started. I'm paying for it so he can get his act together."

"That's good. I hope it works out."

"You hope it works out?" said Rick.

"Of course I do. Do you think I'm that much of a rat fink that I wouldn't?"

"It's just that—"

"Rick, I don't want to see anyone else hurt because of this. If Dabney's innocent, then great. I'm glad. But in the meantime, we can't afford to take any chances. We've got to follow up on the evidence, wherever that might lead us. Do you understand?"

Rick sighed, "Yeah, sure. They'll let him go, don't you think?"

I smiled, "Probably."

We sat there in silence for some time before Chief Hanscom appeared.

"Mr. Hughes, may we speak with you a moment?"

Rick glanced at me, confused as to why they would want him. "Why, certainly, Chief."

I was alone again for some time before Walt came by and sat down.

"How did it go?" I asked.

"Not too good," said Walt. "Seems that Rick Hughes is sticking up for his brother. He says that Dabney was with him the night of Buffy's and Merritt's deaths."

"But Rick was having dinner with the Cosgroves that night," I objected.

"Well, he says that Dabney was with him before he went to dinner and right after he left. According to the reports, Dabney couldn't possibly have murdered both those people and proceed to carry off Buffy's body during the time that Rick was having dinner."

"I see. So, where were they supposed to be that night?"

"Before dinner, Rick says that he was at Dabney's house. Afterwards, his story is that they both went to the Montauk Lighthouse where they have a kind of hideaway and spent the night there. Dabney was never out of his sight until the next morning is Rick's story."

"They were on bad terms, not even speaking, is how I remember them,"I countered.

"I don't know, Liz. We questioned them separately and their stories match," Chief Hanscom noted mildly.."

"Which just means they had time to talk about it before you interrogated them."

"Maybe. Or maybe they're telling the truth. Anyway, there's not enough evidence to hold Dabney here, so we had to let him go."

"Wait a second. Aren't you going to wait for the analysis of those clothing fibers?"

Hanscom shook his head. "The lab's backed up with work. We won't get the results until tomorrow, and we can't justify keeping Dabney here that long. But don't worry. They're still suspects in the investigation, and we've made it very clear they're not to leave the East End until the case is closed."

"Great," I said sardonically. "At least we've got them contained, I guess. Maybe I should have expected Rick would lie for his brother, but I didn't figure him for that kind of person."

"Are you that sure he's lying?"

I looked squarely at Walt, "Pretty sure."

All of our leads had led us into dead ends. I couldn't think of anything else to do at the moment, except wait for the lab results, so Walt took me home. Once I lay down, oblivion! Awake at early dawn, I put on a robe and went into the living room, where I found Walt asleep on the couch.

"Come on, sleepy head. Rise and shine."

Having worked in Mexico, I believe in the energy-producing qualities of hot salsa. So, determined to see some action, I brewed some extra strong coffee and turned out a powerful version of huevos rancheros.

We ate at a fireman's clip --I always kidded Walt that it was a good thing he was a cop instead of a fireman since he was a slow eater while I was usually finished by the time he had gotten started.

We left companionably together, winked at the Sobotkas next door and were about to pull away when a police car stopped us. A uniformed man came up to Herrick, saluted and handed him a small parcel.

"I found this brooch," he reported. 'It was on the sand, not far from where Mrs. Cosgrove's body was found."I didn't touch it, of course. Just picked it up with a handkerchief, and wrapped it in this. Chief Hanscom told me to bring it to you --that you could have it analyzed for prints at the lab."

"Maybe the first tangible lead to the killer," Walt murmured. We went back inside and he dialed the lab in Riverhead.

"Come on, Liz," he said. "Let's get this over to the lab. It looks valuable. Someone must be missing it!"

Without unwrapping it completely and merely glancing at it, we could see that it was a Victorian cameo. But the beautiful lady was wearing a necklace of real diamonds. Her hair was gold and the flowers hanging from her headband appeared to my untrained eye to be real rubies.

We headed for Riverhead, going past Flanders, the ancient Brown cemetery where members of only one family were buried , an old clubhouse, small white churches, and finally reached the County Center where the lab was tucked away in a basement.

Walt handed the package to a white-coated technician, warning him to avoid touching the contents, and we left.

A little later the lab director called us to report that there were no fingerprints. But, Ted Herrick added that he had it appraised, that it was an antique, made in France, worth perhaps $10,000 in view of its age and exquisite craftsmanship.

His expert told him that it looked like something that might have been sold at Tiffany's a long time ago.

Finding jewels in the Hamptons was not unusual. I remember a society hostess sending for a detection outfit after she dropped a diamond earring during a lawn party on First Neck Lane.

The Rockville Center firm never did find her earring, but did find a pearl stickpin and an extremely valuable ruby ring.

"Let's advertise," was my recommendation. Walt agreed that this lure might turn up a suspect. Perhaps whoever killed her actually checked the body--made sure it washed up on the shore--or even towed it in and then--bending over to examine his victim--dropped the brooch. Perhaps, after all, the murderer was a woman!

As the resident writer and former AP correspondent, I knocked out the ad:

FOUND -- Valuable Victorian cameo brooch.
Real diamonds and rubies on gold base.
Phone: 287-1260 for information.

I used my own phone since I had an answering machine. Using the police phone, I feared would cause confusion until a special number was set up--and that would take some time.

Weeks had passed since the first death. I was filing regular reports to the law firm, but wondered how much longer they would employ me if I failed to come up with pay dirt. Buffy Cosgrove's estate would soon be going through probate. Meanwhile, lawyers were paying the help, keeping everything as normal as possible.

The ad ran next day in THE SOUTHAMPTON PRESS and my old friend, Victoria Gardner's SAG HARBOR EXPRESS, which was later to be purchased by Gardiner Cowles of the Cowles Publishing family. "Vicky," though, sensibly arranged to continue residing upstairs, over the Express. Printer's ink is in her veins for sure.

Thursday night Walt and I were reading as soft classical music drifted from across the lake. Sound carries over water. Though the day had started out sunny and ended with a brilliant sunset, fingers of fog were rolling in now. Suddenly the phone jangled. I picked it up, said, "Yes?" and waited.

"Do you have it?" a muffled voice inquired.

"What?" I replied rather stupidly.

"The brooch, the brooch. The ad in the paper," my caller went on. It sounded as though he or she --I couldn't tell which --was speaking through a handkerchief.

How should I work this. It looked as though --at last — I was approaching a solution. The voice was disguised, I was sure.

Yet, "I'll meet you!" I said.

"You'll bring it with you?"

"Yes."

There was something distinctive in the cultured tones. F. Scott Fitzgerald said one time that the rich are different, Hemingway answered they have more money. But Fitzgerald was right. They often have what has been called Scarsdale Lockjaw. This voice had the tones of what used to be called the upper classes. Not from the Bronx, that was sure.

Walt had picked up an extension. I knew he was having the conversation taped. We had set that up ahead of time. A detective with ear phones was in the cellar.

"I want a reward," I said, trying to sound greedy and acquisitive –plus brainless.

My caller was not stupid. He or she asked, "Where did you find it?"

"Oh –on Main Street," I improvised. "You must have dropped it."

"How much do you want?"

"What about $500?"

"Certainly, certainly," the voice agreed, and laughed.

That laugh made me shiver. There was a snarling undercurrent.

Walt handed me a note. It read –"Suggest the college windmill. It's small and confined.""I said, "Could you meet me with the cash at the windmill on the Southampton College campus?"

"No, but if you like windmills, how about the windmill office in Sag Harbor tomorrow night at 9 o'clock? I'll have the cash. You bring my brooch. Come alone or the deal's off!" There was a click. The conversation was over.

This meant that the friendly faculty and student body at Southampton College would not be there to rally around and afford the protection of numbers.

A police car pulled up outside. Chief Hanscom, Detective O'Neill and Findley from the Village police force all came into my cottage which suddenly looked very small.

"We've got a meet and Murphy taped it all," Walt told them. "But we've got to provide backup. This may be very dangerous. The killer sure doesn't want to be recognized and I feel certain that's who our caller is."

That night a heavy fog rolled in from the Atlantic, covering the East End with a nearly impenetrable film, obscuring roads and houses with a white veil of vapor. This was the kind of fog responsible for many of the wrecks on the south shore of Long Island.

Fog has sometimes helped the local population. For instance, exotic roses, laburnums, chestnut, beeches and pear trees in Mecox may date from the wreck of the Louis Phillippe in 1842. Part of its cargo consisted of trees and shrubs. The provident villagers salvaged them and planted them in their own gardens.

I prayed that this fog would also prove a help,- and not an obstacle, to finally learning the identity of a vicious murderer.

I dressed in black, hoping that if the caller was armed, I would not present the perfect target in white. As I pulled on the black silky outfit I usually thought of as my funeral dress, I hoped it was not an omen of my own funeral.

My pearl-handled gun, a legacy from my late husband, was slipped into a brocade bag and I was ready.

We stopped at the Village police headquarters on Main Street to let them know we were heading out to Sag Harbor. A cop who was to marry a millionaire's daughter in a few years was studying the social register. Southampton may be on of the few areas in the world where a copy of the listing of blue bloods is kept in the Police Department's file as standard operating procedure.

After dinner at the American Hotel, we headed for the windmill at the foot of Main Street and the entrance to Long Wharf.

A few couples were out on the wharf , but due to the fog there wasn't much traffic.

I could hear a love song drifting over from a nearby anchored yacht.

It was about a quarter to nine. Walt and a few other policemen waved before disappearing.

"I'll be right nearby, Liz," Walt promised before vanishing into the fog.

Keeping a sharp lookout for whoever had called, I stood in the doorway of the windmill, used during the season as a Chamber of Commerce operation and gorgeously arrayed in colored lights at Christmas time. Though I was trying hard to watch for any movement, the attack took me totally by surprise. Whoever it was grabbed me from behind –circling my neck with strong fingers.

"Where's the brooch?"

I couldn't speak so the fingers relaxed their hold enough for me to mumble, "In my left-hand pocket."

Holding on with one hand, he or she felt around my jacket and took the tiny package. planted there, a rough facsimile, not the original. I broke away and headed down the wharf. I could see nothing, but the sound of fog horns made me sure I was going towards the end of the wharf.

As I ran I opened my bag, getting out the gun. But before I could fire it, I was in the waters of Sag Harbor Cove. A strong hand had pushed me over. And followed me over into the water. Like almost all locals, I have always been a strong swimmer. Obviously, so was the killer. Again, my throat was encircled by those powerful hands.

"That's not my mother's brooch, you bitch," the raspy voice yelled at me. I fought back, grabbing the hands, kicking and trying to break loose. In between, we both went down and then sprang up to the surface again. The last time down seemed longer. I was starting to black out, still holding onto my attacker in a double death grip. If I drowned, he would drown with me in the drowning person's fatal hold. Just when I thought we were going down for good, something exploded nearby.

"Are you OK, Liz? Where are you?" It was Walt, bless him. Soon the cove was full of swimming cops. Surrounding me, they separated me from my partner in our aquatic ballet.

Feeling like a soaking bundle of wet clothes, I shook myself like a dog when I got onto the wharf, having been pulled up to terra firma by a uniformed Sag Harbor cop. He seemed to be the only dry person on the pier. A black form, equally wet, came next. The face was invisible due to the fog and apparently a dark hood.

John Harrington, in that era a seemingly permanent fixture of the old whaling town's police force, snapped handcuffs on the prone figure. He then pulled back the hood and shone his flashlight into the wet face of Richard Hughes.

"Impossible!" I said to Walt.

"You have the brooch," a weak voiced Hughes murmured. "It was my mother's. She always loved him. Always." His voice died out.

Walt listened to his heart for a few moments. I silently handed him a mirror from my bag. He held it next to Hughes mouth. There was no moisture on the glass. Richard Hughes was dead.

It took us a while to work it all out.

We learned later that he had a weak heart, greatly worsened by his worthless brother's drug addiction. Dabney, of course, had stolen Cindy's wallet. His cocaine habit killed his brother's business and ruined his prospects for marrying Buffy Cosgrove who wasn't about to marry someone beneath her socially, who also, worse yet, was a pauper.

The two brothers were the product of an adulterous affair between a wealthy socialite and their mother, Meg Kazlow, the daughter of a Southampton milkman, Ziggy Kazlow. The brooch was a gift from the rich man who kept his mistress well. But when his wife died, he refused to marry Meg Kazlow. A true Polish beauty, she married Alan Hughes while the boys were small and he brought them up as his sons. Her depressions continued after his death until her final commitment to a hospital for the mentally ill, a heartbreaking climax.

Richard grew up hating the Dune Road residents whom he saw often as his grandfather delivered their milk and he waited in the truck. Like other Southampton kids, he also worked summers, caddying at the Meadow Club, and serving drinks at the Southampton Bathing Corporation and saw close up the enormous barrier erected between the classes, as rigid in America as any in England.

He studied hard, got a scholarship to Yale, passed the SEC tests, but never got over his bitter sorrow over his mother's tragedy.

His romance with Buffy Cosgrove seemed promising and he was even relaxing a little from his hatred for the rich and well-born until she learned that she would be excluded from the listings of society, possibly even be blackballed from some of her clubs if she married another nobody. Rafael, though a sponge, was possessed of a title from an obscure European republic and so she remained in the register during her years as his wife. But to marry Hughes, a local milkman's grandson, would have meant expulsion. Though not really a snob, Buffy couldn't face the prospect.

She had told him her decision the very night she was murdered. She also told him that Millie had warned her, summing up, "He has no real money or background, you know. I think his folks were from some armpit of the universe --some place like Passaic or Paterson, New Jersey, or Queens."

This explained his grudge against Millie Darlington. But it seemed likely that Richard Hughes, had he lived, might have gotten off on a temporary insanity plea since he seemed to have gone completely over the edge, killing Rhinelander Merritt just for being in the register, and apparently, from the list found among his papers, preparing to kill others on the list.

The committee heads of the past may have influenced his father's decision against marrying his mistress and the mother of his two sons, but it all happened so long ago that only an unbalanced mind would have kept the grudge alive.

As for me, I sent in a final report to the law firm, got my last check, and resumed my quiet round of activities at Little Fresh Pond.

The summer was drawing to an end. A solemn row of Rolls Royces and limousines was heading south for Palm Beach. I waved to Thomas Jefferson who was piloting his long, shiny black limousine, with an aged dowager in the back seat, southward. Paul Ward went by and got another wave. Favorite Southampton cabbies make the trip between Southampton and Palm Beach at the beginning and end of every season.

One night during Labor Day weekend, Walt and I went to the acreage next to the North Sea Community House for the North Sea Fire Department's end of season carnival.

A huge American flag rose in the sky, perfect in every detail. Irma Mertlich's brother, Erik Sachtleben, was setting off the fireworks display for the folks who live on the wrong side of the railroad tracks, as Herb McCarthy, owner of Bowden Square, once described North Sea to a visitor.

Skyrockets burst over the ocean on the other end of town. A gorgeous bouquet of gold, carmine and dawn pink roses filled the night sky. The Southampton Bathing Corporation or maybe the Meadow Club was also marking the end of another summer season in the Hamptons.

At the Shinnecock Reservation, the annual Labor Day Pow Wow was underway. Indians from all over America were providing Indian dances and other traditional entertainment on the reservation with its memorial to the ten Shinnecock Indians who perished in the wreck of the Circassian off Mecox in 1876.

Three separate worlds in one small town, billed as the oldest English settlement in New York, founded in 1640.

(While Gardiners Island was ceded to Lion Gardiner a year before, in 1639, by Charles I and Wyandance, the sachem of the Montauks, the enchanted island has always been more of a fief or kingdom, owned by the Gardiner family, than a settlement. So, Southampton does deserve its claim—*perhaps!*)

▼

EPILOGUE

Many changes have come about following the death of Richard Hughes and the solution of the Society Murders as some tabloids dubbed them. Thanks to the publicity, I am not lacking for business.

The Planning Board chairman was recently found with his throat cut in his office on Hampton Road. I have been retained by the Town Board to aid in the investigation. Walt has been permitted by Sag Harbor police and Southampton Town Police Chief Hanscom to work with me. Irate conservationists are suspected.

Walt and I are still dear friends, but marriage is still off on the horizon. Maybe we're happier this way.

Mrs. Ary Dault did leave Southampton forever. She said that not only had the blue bloods rejected her beloved "Lub," but the locals had been rude to him at the last General Election, keeping him waiting in line at the VFW Clubhouse. She and Jamie, her most recent pug dog, left us forever via Stanley and the East Hampton Airport. She is believed to be traveling from island to island by hydroplane.

THE END

▼

www.ingramcontent.com/pod-product-compliance
Lightning Source LLC
Chambersburg PA
CBHW020024030726
47499CB00007B/2262